One Dark Body

Also by Charlotte Watson Sherman

Killing Color

One Dark Body

A NOVEL

Charlotte Watson Sherman

HarperCollins*Publishers*

"Floating" appeared as a short story in *Killing Color*, published by Calyx Books in 1992.

HarperCollins books may be purchased for educational, business, or sales promotional use. For information, please write: Special Markets Department, HarperCollins Publishers, Inc., 10 East 53rd Street, New York, NY 10022.

FIRST EDITION

Designed by Alma Hochhauser Orenstein

Library of Congress Cataloging-in-Publication Data
Sherman, Charlotte Watson, 1958–
    One dark body: a novel/Charlotte Watson Sherman. —1st ed.
        p.   cm.
    ISBN 0-06-016924-9
    I. Title.
PS3569.H41505   1993
813'.54—dc20   92-53342

93 94 95 96 97 ❖/HC 10 9 8 7 6 5 4 3 2 1

For David

CONTENTS

▼

Acknowledgments   ix
Prologue   1
Floating   3
Crows   27
Things Handed Down   49
The Space Between Words Where People Live   73
Blood Memory   99
The Color of Spirits   123
Soulcatcher   137
One Dark Body   161
Epilogue   205

ACKNOWLEDGMENTS

▼

Many people have influenced and helped this novel find its finished form: my editor, Stephanie Gunning, my agent, Beth Vesel, my attorney and friend, Kevin Davis, Nancy Rawles, Tina Hoggatt, Leonore Norgaard, and especially my spirit guides, Brenda Peterson, Perry Ullander, and David Sherman.

I am grateful for the support and friendship of Carletta Wilson, Barbara Henderson, Faith Davis, JoAnn Moton, Julia Boyd, Jody Kim, Rick Simonson, and Barbara Thomas; Colleen McElroy and Calyx Books Collective; and Red and Black Books Collective.

I'd like to thank my family: Charles Watson, Dorothy and Harold Glass, Alton Sherman, Josh and Kitty Gardner, Erika Sherman, Richard Glass, Michael Glass, and Lois Sherman for being there for my daughters when I could not.

x ▼ ONE DARK BODY

For their patience and love, I am eternally grateful to David, Aisha, and Zahida Sherman.

And for the music: Sweet Honey in the Rock, Esther "Littledove" John, Miriam Makeba, Bobbie McFerrin, SunRa and his Intergalactic Orkestra, and Miles Davis.

One ever feels his twoness, —an American, a negro; two souls, two thoughts, two unreconciled strivings; two warring ideals in one dark body, whose dogged strength alone keeps it from being torn asunder.

—W. E .B. DuBois,
THE SOULS OF BLACK FOLK

PROLOGUE

▼

Wasn't nobody near the hushed water that time of night to see or hear the body move itself up from the hole in the bottom of the lake, through the opaque water, and past the lake's upside where it floated dark and fluid as the little sea itself.

The dark body moved silkily on the water, a shadowy milk, growing, moving simply, offering no resistance, but easing on, gracefully riding the waves.

Old and new ribbons of algae twisted about the torso like banners, waving surely, softly too, toward the edge of the lake that rose from the water itself darker even than this moonless night.

▼▼▼▼▼▼▼▼▼▼▼▼▼▼▼▼▼▼▼▼▼▼▼▼▼

SECTION 1

Floating

▲▲▲▲▲▲▲▲▲▲▲▲▲▲▲▲▲▲▲▲▲▲▲▲▲

I

Raisin 1963

▼

THIS A FUNNY PLACE. Maybe cause of the mountain standing up behind our town watching like a big old eye. Or maybe it's that lake stretching way out, reaching black to black, pushing its way cross the earth like it's in a hurry to run away from here. Or maybe it's that twisted-trunk, yellow-leaf tree next to Blue-the-wanga-man's house, with the leaves that shine like gold lamps through the trees, day or night.

But some folks say no, it's not that mountain sitting back watching over us, and it's not that black lake reaching, and it's not that old white-trunked, yellow-tipped tree next to Blue's that Reverend Daniles swears covers a hole leading from this world to the next. The thing that makes Pearl a funny kind of place is all that whispering we hear coming up from the ground.

I first heard it one day when I was walking with Miss Marius from her house to town.

Even though the only place I ever lived was in her house, I

never thought of her house as mine. And don't nobody else think no different from me.

My mama left Pearl soon as I was born, years before the last coal mine closed down and lots of colored folks left town. Folks from Mississippi, Georgia, Louisiana, Alabama. Come all the way to Washington to shake that red dirt off their feet, get those red fingers off their souls. Miss Marius always say, "You can run to the new South, but you can't hide from the old South, not even way out here."

But I remember when I was back in my mama's stomach, floating like a pickle in a jar. I remember what was said, the bargains struck.

I could hear them talking while I was floating, sitting in all that water.

A high dark sound, my mama's laughing and crying and a long, sharp tone, smooth as the knife Miss Marius used to cut meat from bone. I remember Miss Marius talking, talking, saying the same words over and over till my mama's cry turned into a stretched-out moan.

And Miss Marius going around in the water with me. Going around in the tart, dark liquid. The low sound of her voice stroking me inside that bag, inside that wineskin where I floated in a dream.

"What did you take, Nola? What did you put up inside yourself, child? Tell me. I'm gonna help you and I'm gonna help this baby, too, but you got to tell me what you put into yourself. I got most of the okra out, but what else? What was it, Nola? Was it something from inside the house, something from the woods?"

And Miss Marius and my mama went around, circling till my mama, exhausted, let the words fall from her lips like some hard, funny-shaped stones. "Blue told me to use cedar berries and camphor," she said, and that's all I remember from when I was in my mama's stomach. But folks don't know I even remember that, not even Miss Marius, cause them first years Miss Marius's deep voice and big-knuckled hands was all the mama I thought I'd need.

"Hush that foolishness, child," Miss Marius always say. "Everybody needs they mama and you got one just like everybody else. She'll be back when she gets a notion."

But it scared me when Miss Marius talk like that. I don't know if I like my mama's notions. The very first one she ever took about me left me shriveled up and gasping inside her womb.

That's why I come out looking so old and wrinkled everybody took to calling me Raisin. But I don't think it's the wrinkles that make me look old. I think it's like Miss Marius says, I'm an old old soul.

We live out on the edge of town on the east side, where all the colored people live. Miss Marius's house is the last one you come to fore you hit all them trees and marsh at the edge of the lake, out where old Blue lives.

We live in what used to be an old rooming house. We got a downstairs and a front room and a kitchen with a big black stove.

Upstairs is where we all sleep. Miss Marius and Nathan in the big room at the front of the house with that window letting in all the light from the world.

Miss Marius and Nathan got no children of they own, but Lucille and Lucinda are sisters and they act like they the ones come outta Miss Marius's body, even though Miss Marius say we all her children. Since they been here the longest, longer than my twelve years, they both get to sleep in that room big enough to be a play yard, with all them goop-de-goos they got spread out all around the floor. They both got white-painted beds with flowers all scrolled around they heads so when they laying in em, it's like they laying inside a wreath, kind of like a halo around their heads.

I sleep with MC and Wilhelmina and Douglass in the back bedroom, in that big old brown bed that we climb up onto with a stool. It be tight sometimes with all us squeezed up in it, but I'm just glad I don't have to share the bed with Lucille.

Lucille gonna be big, just like Miss Marius. She got a thick-waisted body and short, strong legs. Her neck's thick too, and strong enough for all the yelling she think she gotta do. She like to drop her head back and yell loud as she can.

Her hair ain't black and thick like mine, it's the color of a tree trunk and her eyes the color of moonstone.

One time at supper, I made the mistake of trying to tell her how pretty I thought her eyes was, but she raised herself up like a rattler in her chair and hissed, "Shut your mouth, you old wrinkled-up raisin, fore I put you in a box and sell you to Miss Lomax to eat."

Everybody at the table laugh when she say that, they scared not to. But Miss Marius and Nathan never crack a smile.

I didn't mind. Whenever they start talking about how wrinkled up and black I am, I just close my eyes and think of a warm soft place like a tub of hot water I can lay my body down in, or a nice dark space like a womb.

Lucille say don't nobody love MC, Wilhelmina, Douglass, and me, and that's how come we living with Miss Marius and Nathan. MC ain't nuthin but a baby, so it always make him cry when she say that, but Wilhelmina, Douglass and me all about the same size, so we don't cry, we just look at her.

"Your mamas left you on Miss Marius's porch like a sack of bad-luck pennies. Ain't nobody ever gonna love you," she liked to say, knowing nobody try to talk about how her own mama left her and Lucinda.

When she say that I think of the time Douglass stuck his hand in a bucket of snakes and pull out three so I won't have to, like Lucille was trying to make me do. And Douglass about as scared of snakes as me.

Douglass's mama took all her children but him back to Memphis a while after the mine closed. She left him with Miss Marius so he'd be in good hands.

"That boy slow, Miss Marius. Look at the way that eye jumps, the way he rocks on his feet. He can't make it on this long trip. Can he stay with you till I get settled? I'll send for him soon as I do."

Miss Marius say, "I'll keep him till you ready, Louisa. Y'all go on and make your home."

Wilhelmina's mama did her about the same as mine did me, cept she use a wire to try to get Wilhelmina out, but it didn't work.

"She a special child, Leona, that's why she here. Leave her with me. I'll take care of her," Miss Marius say.

Wilhelmina got a mark, look like a blue moon setting on her face. I think about how she sit with MC, humming soft as water in his ear the times he sound like there's a hole in him so deep nuthin but water could fill it up.

I think about the way we sleep, four brown spoons with our arms around each other. And I look at Lucille when she say don't nobody love us.

I look at her mean as that goat Miss Marius call Moses on account of his white beard hanging down to the ground. I look at her mean as Moses look at us and I say, "No, you lying, Lucille. Somebody do love us."

And I don't even flinch when she grab me by the two plaits Miss Marius wove into my head, I don't even yell when she pull out the weave and swing my plaits to the ground.

I only remember the time I was over to Miss Lomax's house when she first got her new TV and out of the blue glowing in the screen I saw a cowboy jump out of a box and dig his heels into a horse's sides. The man jumped off the horse and grabbed a cow by the horns and tried to drag the cow down to the ground.

And when Lucille swung me down by my braids into the dirt, just like that cowboy roped that cow, I jumped up with a wild look still in my eyes and say, "You're still lying." But my legs were turning like wheels on the road.

I I

▼

THIS MY SECRET PLACE. My green, green holy place, inside this circle of red cedar trees, next to that big-leaf maple with moss that clings to it like smooth green skin.

Even the ground is green and covered with leaves, leaves my teacher Miss Dubois say is called oxalis. I put one of the leaves in my mouth and taste its juicy sour, then rub the green softness into my wrinkled skin.

"One day these wrinkles be gone and my skin be smooth and soft as these leaves. One day it will," I sing into the ears of licorice ferns and salmonberry. Then I lay down to dream on a wild ginger blanket, my smooth, soft second green skin.

A woman comes down the road toward me, a small black bag in one hand. Her eyes are knives and she is not smiling.

Behind her is a bright gray cloud. It is raining white balls, but she is not wet. The woman's arms reach for me, brown and unwrinkled. She opens her mouth, but no sound comes out. I turn from her and run toward the black lake. The woman is behind me, running. She is fast, almost faster than me. I run to the edge of the lake, look back at her reaching hands, her mouth opened like an O. I jump.

The water's coolness soothes me, then starts to burn. I call for help, but she is the only one there, standing, waiting at the edge. My head slips below the surface. I scream as I go down.

"Wake up, girl. What's wrong with you?"

I open my eyes and see Sin-Sin standing over me. He's the color of that stone Miss Dubois got on her desk, Brazilian agate. His skin so bright it shines.

"What are you doing in my secret place, Sin-Sin?"

"This ain't your secret place," Sin-Sin say. "It ain't nobody's secret place cause it ain't even no secret. I walk around back here all the time. So does Blue."

"I never saw neither one of you down here before and I always come down here."

"Well, so do we. What you doing falling asleep out in the woods, girl? Don't you know all kinds of things be out here waiting on somebody like you?"

Sin-Sin ain't but fourteen, so I know he don't have to talk like I ain't got good sense.

"Ain't nuthin out here waiting on me no more than it waiting on you. How come you walking around down here?" I ask.

"To get away from my mama," he say.

"What you want to get away from Miss Dubois for? She nice."

"That's cause she ain't your mama. She was, you'd be running down here hiding, too."

"I wish my mama was a schoolteacher," I say.

"That's cause you ain't never lived with a schoolteacher

mama before, that's all. Once you get a taste of all the books she make you read, you be glad you got the mama you got."

"Miss Marius my mama."

"That right? I thought she Lucille and Lucinda's mama."

"She is, sort of. She our mama, too: me and Wilhelmina and MC and Douglass, she our mama, too."

"Your mamas left all of you for Miss Marius to keep?" he ask.

"Uh huh," I say back.

"You're lucky. Mamas are hard on you, making you work all the time around the house, and read all the time and study figures and wash your hands fore you come in the kitchen and always wanting you to clean your ears. And they don't want you to talk like you want to talk. I wish mine would leave me with Miss Marius."

"Miss Marius alright. I can't stand Lucille. Always act like a razor in her mouth," I say.

"She's big. Don't nobody mess with Lucille."

"I told her she a lie, right to her face," I say.

"You did?"

"Yep."

"That must be why you hiding in the woods. Lucille gonna get you good for saying that."

"She ain't gonna get me cause I ain't going back there. I'm gonna stay here and live in these woods," I tell him.

"How you gonna eat and get clean clothes?"

"I'm gonna eat salmonberries and mushrooms. And I'll make some dresses and pants out of leaves."

"What about school? My mama's gonna want you to do your homework. She don't care where you live."

"You could bring my books to me out here. And I could give you my schoolwork for Miss Dubois," I say.

"My mama don't want me mixed up in no trouble. She say plenty trouble waiting in the world for me later on."

"I ain't talking about getting in no trouble. Miss Marius say never trouble trouble till trouble troubles you, but she usually be talking about white folks," I say. I look in Sin-Sin's face, see the sticks and dirt clotted in his hair, the long red scratch reaching cross one cheek like a streak of lightning, the dry white mud on his blue pants.

"You going around looking like that and you worried about getting in trouble for taking my schoolwork to your mama?" I ask. He duck his head.

"I ain't never known you to be scared of no trouble before, Sin-Sin."

"You don't know nuthin about me, girl," he say.

Sin-Sin wrong. I know some things. Heard Miss Marius grumbling, " Ain't nuthin worse than a mind sitting still. Ain't nuthin left for a empty mind to do but worry about other folks' business. Miss Dubois a fine woman. Just what this town needs, and some folks still want to worry over how she got that baby."

Once I hear Miss Lomax say Sin-Sin was the devil's baby. When I ask what she mean, she say on account of his color, that orange-burning red.

"It ain't natural," she say. "What colored folks you know walk around glowing like that?"

I look in Sin-Sin's face now and touch it one time. That soft burning skin. He don't like folks to make much of it, though.

I tell him, "You're used to living inside all that shine. All I got is these old wrinkles."

"They don't look no worse than nuthin else to me. Besides, I like old folks," he say, walking backwards from my secret place, into the fading dark, into the trees.

I go back to Miss Marius's that night. Walk straight up to Lucille and wait. Close my eyes though. I'm too scairt to look death straight in the face.

"Where you been, honey? We already ate, but there's a plate on

the stove you can warm," Miss Marius call out from the front room
where she sit with her eyes closed, letting the day settle in her bones.

I open one of my eyes and look at Lucille. She look at me so
long I open my other eye.

"You ain't got no sense," was all she say before walking into
the front room to sit with Miss Marius.

Then it seem like every time I go to my secret place, Sin-Sin
there. We run through the trees and play explore, picking up
leaves and bugs and mushrooms.

We pull some big sticks and leaves together into something
looking like a shack, but Sin-Sin say it gonna be a tree house like
he read about in a book his mama give him.

"We can't call it that, cause I ain't climbing up in them trees,"
I tell him so he can hurry and get that thought out of his head.
These trees around here big and tall, go back a long, long way, clear
back to what Miss Dubois call Lewis and Clark. He poke out his lips
a bit, but we still don't put that house up in them trees.

We find two big rocks for chairs and a piece of log for a
table. Most times we just sit inside and tell stories.

"I asked Miss Marius where the Night People come from and
she say they always been here. She say one time she saw the
Night People down here," I say.

"What she say they look like?" Sin-Sin ask.

"Just like everybody say, tall as some of these trees, snake-
haired and yellow-eyed," I say. "That's how she saw one cause its
eyes was glowing in the dark and she thought it was a cat way up
in the branches, but when she heard it whistle, she knew it
wasn't no kind of cat."

"What was Miss Marius doing out in the woods at night? You
can't see no Night People unless you out here at night," Sin-Sin
say. "She out in the woods looking for Blue? My mama said Miss
Marius and Blue was friends when they was young."

"No. She wasn't looking for no wanga-man. She out here looking for Miss Buchanan."

"That lady walk around all the time talking to herself and stay out by the dump?"

"Miss Marius say that how she got like she got. When they was girls they was friends and Miss Buchanan was alright then.

"But one day she got it in her head to run off to the woods cause her mama had died and her daddy wouldn't stop acting like he was crying all the time, even after her mama had been dead for a long time, and Miss Buchanan couldn't take it no more cause she thought her daddy would've liked it better if she was the one to go, which wasn't true, Miss Marius say, but the girl wasn't thinking right by then, so she took off.

"Miss Marius thought she knew about where Miss Buchanan had hid herself, so she set off to go get her. Well, after she walked way up in here, she thought she'd gotten lost, which was funny for her cause she thought she knew these woods like the back of her hand, even in the dark.

"It was about then she looked up and seen them two shining yellow eyes in a tree. She thought it was a cat, but then she saw it shake its head side to side real slow and she saw them snakey ropes swing around. She couldn't make out no arms or legs, so she thought it must be sitting up in the tree.

"Then it turned them yellow eyes on a spot back of Miss Marius and start whistling. She say it don't sound like nuthin from this world. She still don't move a muscle, cause she think it might suck her up in them trees or something. So she stay still while she look in them eyes.

"She say it seem like something was being passed on to her while she was looking in them eyes, seem like she feel a humming in her body.

"Then she heard a moan coming from somewhere behind her. She turn her head to try to see exactly where the moan was coming from and then she hear a whirring sound and turn her head back to them eyes, but they was gone.

"She move over to the moaning and find Miss Buchanan laying on some moss. She didn't never say nuthin that made sense no more."

"I bet they put a spell on her. That's what they supposed to do if they catch you out in they woods at night," Sin-Sin say.

"Miss Marius say she never did go back in them woods at night no more and she told us we better do the same."

"Well, all I know is, I'm not scared of no Night People whistling and carrying on," Sin-Sin say.

"What you gonna do if one sees you? Them people carry spears and can fly. What you gonna do if you come up against one of them?" I ask.

"Blue say Night People only bother people who bother them or theirs. He say they ain't nuthin but old ones who've gone before us."

"What he mean?"

"He mean Night People ain't nuthin but spirits."

"Spirits . . . like ghosts?"

"Yeah. People that are there, but we just can't see them. Blue say spirits around us all the time."

I look outside our house into the listening trees. I hear birds talking, leaves brushing against each other. I look at Sin-Sin's eyes shining in the light and I know I ain't gonna tell no more stories about Night People.

One time, after I tell all the stories for about a week and Sin-Sin don't say too much of anything one way or the other, I decide I ain't gonna tell another story till he take his turn. So we pick more leaves and grass for our roof for a while and then come inside our house and sit down. Sin-Sin wiggle for a while on his chair, but I still don't say a mumbling word. He finally sit still and look at me with a face that older than mine.

"The Night People come for me one time," he say and wrap his skinny arms around hisself and start to rock his body side to side like Douglass do to calm hisself.

"What you say?" I ask.

He close his eyes and I lean up close to his face to hear.

"They come for me once and say they gonna come back."

Sin-Sin look like I feel thinking about the Night People coming anywhere for me.

"They come to your house?" I ask.

Sin-Sin nod his head, slow-like.

"Come right inside and got in my bed, climbed right inside my head."

"Huh?"

"I was dreaming. I was standing near the edge of the lake. Could hear the sound of water licking the rocks. Could hold out my hand and touch the lumps on a white stick laying on the bank like a long broken arm. The air smelled like mud.

"It wasn't real. The waves was moving like a million mouths opening their lips and talking. Talking to me.

"I stepped up, close to the edge as I could get without putting my feet in the water. The black water in that lake turned orange as a tangerine.

"I felt my daddy in there.

"I put one foot in the water and the talking mouths pulled me in and I fell inside that water and floated in the dream. Didn't hear nuthin but whispers. The shushing of the waves.

"Saw a shape drift by. Something tell me, that's him. That's my daddy. I follow the shape. Move my body in the water like it do. Something hold me. Something grab my arm, turn me round. Push something solid in my mouth. I swallow. My mouth taste like rock.

"I turn my head toward the shape I think is my daddy, but he gone. The mouths, the waves tell me to hush. They hold me by my arms and rock me. Sing me a song but I can't understand the words.

"I try to say, I want my daddy. I want to go with him, but they say no. I get mad. I say no and try to get away, but red wings fly toward me in the water. I feel a huge bird grab hold of my shoulders and lift me. Then I am leaving the lake, the dark orange water, the place where I felt my daddy.

"The bird take me up in the woods to a circle of tall, snake-haired trees.

"The trees whistle and open they arms. The bird drop me in the middle of the circle and fly away, red wings glowing in the dark.

"In they whistle-talk they tell me to climb inside the trunk of the oldest tree, say I should wait inside there.

"I climb inside the white-walled hole and look out into the yellow-eyed night. I call on my daddy cause I feel scared.

"The trees keep whistling as they cover the hole and seal me inside the darkness."

Sin-Sin crying when he finish his story, long salty tears that move down his face leaving slug trails. The only boy I ever seen cry was MC and he ain't nuthin but a baby.

I don't know what to do with Sin-Sin's tears. So I pick up a leaf and smooth it on his face.

"It ain't nuthin but a dreamstory, Sin-Sin. Nuthin but a dream," I say while I smooth the salt into his orange skin.

"I ain't never gonna know nuthin about my daddy," he whisper.

He turn his head and look at me close.

"You ain't never gonna tell nobody about the dream, is you?"

"What I want to tell that for?" I ask back.

"You gotta promise," he say.

"Alright."

"No, I mean you really gotta promise. We gotta seal it with blood."

I look at him close and say, "I ain't sealing nuthin with no blood."

"Alright. A kiss then. A soul-kiss," he say.

"What a soul-kiss?" I ask.

"Here. I'll show you," he say.

Sin-Sin lean up against my face and put his lips against mine. I smell the green from the leaf in his face. It smell like green water. He push his tongue in my mouth. I start to bite, but don't. Sin-Sin taste like salt. He pull his tongue out like a snake sucking in.

"That's a soul-kiss," he say, not looking old no more. "That's as good as a bloodseal."

I ain't thinking about Sin-Sin and his crazy story. All I think about is telling Lucille I got something she say I ain't never gonna get.

"Whatcha'll doing in there?"

We jump back in our seats at the sound of Blue's voice. Sin-Sin know him, I don't. All I know is stories I been told.

"Blue a wanga man," Lucille told me one time. "You know what that is?"

"No," I say as she pinch my arm.

"It's a man can turn hisself into a snake or a lizard or a goat. Anything he want, he can change into."

"How you know?" I ask.

"I heard some of the grown folks talking," Lucille say. "They say didn't nobody know nuthin about Blue, he just up and was one day. Miss Lomax's brother say he saw him coming up from the lake, no boat, no car, no nuthin. He just come walking into town from the lake. And you know there's only marsh and trees by the lake. I bet he turned hisself into a fish, got tired of the water, and then turned hisself into a man and come up on land to walk like the rest of us."

I didn't believe her then. Now, I don't say nuthin. Just look at the beads and shells around Blue's neck. He got a piece of glass hanging on a neck rope, shining. When I look inside the glass, everything new and shaped funny.

I wonder if that's how he do his changing. Stretch out and fall deep inside his bones. Blood shifting around like sand till he's new.

He twist his head in my direction, then turn his long neck to Sin-Sin.

"You remember what I told you, boy?" he ask.

Sin-Sin nod his head, but don't look in Blue's eyes.

"Soon as you ready, you come see me. You hear?" he say.

Sin-Sin don't say nuthin. He keep his eyes on the floor of our treehouse-on-the-ground.

Blue grunt, then he gone.

"What he talking about, Sin-Sin? You fooling around with a wanga man?"

"You believe whatever folks tell you, don't you?" he ask.

"Don't you?"

"No. I like to find things out for myself. Plenty of times grown folks are wrong about things," he say.

"They wrong about Blue?" I ask. "He ain't no wanga?"

"He's a man that knows some things, things most folks are bound to forget."

"He don't open up a chicken's neck and drink its blood?" I ask. "He can't turn into a snake and make your mama's heart stop beating if you look at him crosseyes?"

"Your mama's heart need to stop if you walking around looking at folks crosseyed. Blue ain't no fool."

"What you doing messing around with him? I bet Miss Dubois don't like that!" I say.

"He say he can teach me things, things I won't learn in no books."

"What kind of things?" I ask.

"Things he say'll help me grow into a man, things my mama don't know nuthin about."

"He seem alright," I say.

"He is alright. He serious is all."

"Is that why he don't smile at folks in town?" I ask.

"He thinks that's shining, shining for white folk, and he ain't never gonna do that. Blue say he stopped smiling the day they run his daddy into the river cause his daddy hurt the white man who hurt Blue's mama. And down in Mississippi, they was like most of the colored people up here. Couldn't none of em swim. They never found his daddy's body.

"Blue say he keeps that picture in the front of his mind: his daddy running out of the house and down the road, the high round behinds of the horses chasing him, running him down to the river and in.

"Blue followed the trail of red dust the horses left behind. Then he hid in some bushes by the river and watched. He watched his daddy fall in the fast white water. Then he saw him stand with his legs shaking, but his back straight as he walked farther into the water, till all Blue could see was bubbles where his daddy's head had been. Blue stopped talking then. He didn't talk for five or six years."

"He tell you that?" I ask.

"How else I'm gonna know?"

"What he want with you?"

Sin-Sin duck his head like he do when Blue come. He sit still for a while with his forehead wrinkled bad as mine, then his skin smooth out and he shake his shoulders like he coming out of a dream.

"He's gonna cut me," he say.

"What?"

"He's gonna give me a man-cut, cut me like they used to do to make you into a man."

"You crazy?" I ask. "What you wanna let him cut on you for? Your mama know about him cutting on you? I bet she don't. I bet this something you and Blue made up."

"No, it's real. He showed me a picture of it in a book he got."

"Blue cutting on you is gonna be your behind, I bet."

"My mama ain't never gonna know," he say.

"What?" I ask.

"I ain't gonna tell her. This something women don't know nuthin about. He's gonna ask my mama to let me spend some time with him and that's when he's gonna do it. He's been telling me things I'm gonna need to know so I can be ready."

"How come you can't just be a man like everybody else? How come you gotta get cut?"

"So I can leave childish things behind and be a grown man, Blue say."

"Is that all you think about, being a grown man?" I ask him, frowning.

"What else I'm gonna think about?" he ask, frowning too.

"You better think about that cutting some more. And do some thinking about your mama. I know Miss Dubois ain't gonna stand for nuthin like this," I say.

All he say is, "She can't make me into a man. Blue can.".

I I I

▼

THAT THE LAST TIME I see Sin-Sin in our treehouse for a while. I see him in school some time, but he turn his head like he don't wanna see me.

I try to tell him one more time I won't tell Miss Dubois or nobody else. We could make a soul-kiss if he want. But he turn from me whenever he see me coming, like he turning from something evil in a dream.

I don't mind. I keep on going to my secret place, sitting inside the treehouse and telling stories to myself.

After a while, I stop worrying about Sin-Sin and his secrets cause Miss Marius got a note from a woman saying she my mama.

I bring it out here and puzzle over it sometime. Feel the loop-de-loop of Miss Marius's name on the paper and the other strange, dangerous name.

Dear Miss Marius,
    Things sure do change, so do people. What goes around comes around in a hurry they say. I'm coming around there for my child.
    Please accept these few dollars as my thanks. The words'll have to wait till I come.

Nola Barnett
1653 Cottage Grove South
Chicago, Illinois

Miss Marius say this my mama. And Nola Barnett say she coming here to get me.

That's when I first heard the whispers, the ones coming up from the ground. Heard a man voice and a woman, too. The man keep calling me, calling me his baby girl.

Me and Miss Marius was walking to the depot for the woman that say she my mama. We pass by Miss Lomax's and see her husband Mr. Lomax sitting with his fiddle between his knees on his porch.

"How y'all doing," he ask.

"Fine, Mr. Lomax," we say. "How you?"

Even Miss Marius call him Mr. Lomax. He long and skinny and like to fuss with Reverend Daniles. Like to call him a jackleg preacher that keep messing with people's minds. When I ask Miss Marius what he talking about, she tell me to stay out of grown folks' foolishness.

"Don't neither one of em know what they talking about," she always say and keep on doing what she be doing.

Miss Lomax say that fiddling belong to the devil, so she get a brand new TV to run so Mr. Lomax won't play. But he still do. Sit right up in the room and fiddle like it the end of the world, Miss Marius say. Even with that TV set on.

Miss Lomax act like she don't hear him, keep right on watching that blue light in the TV. Some nights you can hear them both, the TV and the fiddle going on into the night.

"I gots my fiddle back, so I'm alright," Mr. Lomax say as we pass.

"Somebody took your fiddle, Mr. Lomax?" Miss Marius ask.

"Somebody tried to take it, but I'm too old and smart for that," he laugh as we walk on down the road.

When we on the stretch of road between Miss Lomax's and Miss Dubois's, I hear them.

"What's that?" I ask Miss Marius, who keep on walking down the road.

"What's what?" she ask, still walking.

I stop dead in the middle of the road and listen. "You hear that?"

"I don't hear nuthin but my heart beating in my ears from all this walking," she say. "You better hurry. We don't want to keep your mama waiting."

I don't tell her I wait. All my life and I don't even know I'm waiting. Don't say, let her wait, let her sit there and think about things like I do.

But I keep hearing the voices, they start to build in my ears till I almost scream, but I don't. Miss Marius'd think I don't want to go see Miss Nola that say she my mama.

I don't want to go see her, but it's the whispers that stop me from moving.

The whispers jump up from the ground and settle in my bones till my body gets heavy like a big piece of wood and I'm stuck. A man voice calling, "Baby girl . . . Baby girl, I'm here now, watching over you." My legs take root and I stand in the road with my arms stuck out.

The whispers move through my body, a humming in my

bones that circles round my waist tight as a belt and I can't breathe, can't move, can't even open my mouth to call out to Miss Marius.

"Baby girl. Baby girl," voices say under the whispers. The whispers sound like white-capped water swirling round inside my head till I think I'm gonna fall from the weight, but I don't.

The whispers hold me still and fill up my head with an old watery sound ... WHOOSHBEE ... WHOOSHBEE ... WHOOSHBEE ... WHOOSHBEE ...

SECTION 2

Crows

I

Nola

▼

THE WHINE OF THE TRAIN'S WHISTLE reminded Nola of the red rooster's muted scream so many hard mornings ago. Nola was fifteen when she left Pearl with the echo of that scream burning inside her mind. Fifteen, and sharply focused on a rooster's call so she could forget the open wounds of other scars she was trying to leave behind.

Closing her eyes as the train carried her back to Pearl, Nola remembered how things were twelve years ago, before she had left.

"Nola! Nola! What you doing sleeping in the middle of the day, child? Don't you know we got work to do? The Barneses and Duprees all gonna be coming round here for supper and look at this place! I didn't ask you to help do none of the cooking, but I know you're gonna get off your behind and help clean this house. Didn't you hear that rooster out there? He's been acting crazy all morning, crowing when he should be sleep and sleep when he should be crowing. He about as mixed up as you. Now get up out of that bed before I set it on fire!"

Nola pulled the covers close to her body to protect it from her mother's raving. Her mother's every word landed like a well-placed dart in her belly, growing like a soft dark balloon beneath the sheets.

She knew she was going to get up, but didn't want to shift around too much yet. It would be bad enough when all those people came around. The thought of their probing eyes was enough to stir the queasiness awaiting to disrupt her stomach.

As she lay in bed breathing heavily, she heard the scratching of their red rooster in the dirt outside her window. Ari usually avoided this side of the house, and his aggravated movements were as disturbing to her now as they'd ever been.

CURKACURKACAWWW . . .

Ari's sudden roar made her sit up. This roar did not carry the pride of his usual arrogant cry; this was the scream of an old, fading man.

CURKACURKACAWWW . . .

A rush of nausea forced her to lay down again, but only for a moment. The sound of her mother and the rooster squabbling outside made her get out of bed to watch them through the room's one window.

"Get out of here with all that noise, you old raggedy bird you!" Nola's mother screamed as she chased Ari around the yard, swinging her broom.

Nola knew the strength of her mother's body as well as the swelling of her own. If her mother connected the broom with the bird, a lifetime of fury would put Ari to rest permanently.

Fortunately, Ari, though old, was quick enough to evade the controlled, purposeful blows of Ouida Barnett. Once Nola would have smiled at the picture her mother made meanly sweeping dust in the yard, but now every inch extending the boundary of her growing belly was mortar, cold angry mortar that sealed a wall of silence between her mother and herself. Now there were few smiles between them.

"I don't know when that woman's gonna sit herself down and rest. Look at her. I don't care if she is my sister, she's still a mess, even after all these years," Bess muttered into Nola's ear.

Nola smelled the cutting scent of mint and Jack Daniels. She cupped the bottom of her stomach. Bess rested her hands on the swollen belly too.

"She's gonna come around. Watch and see. Don't none of our people turn our backs on one of our own. She just don't know what to do with herself is all, but she's gonna come around."

"I hope you're right, Bessie. Y'all and this baby's all I got in this world."

"Well, when is El gonna get up his nerve and come on around here and talk to your mama?"

Nola shrugged. She hadn't talked to El since she'd told him he was gonna have to go into Crescent and find a job in the coal mine, a job paying enough money so all three of them could live decent and have food to eat. Her mama had let her know they weren't gonna live in her house.

"I ain't the one told you to lay up and get no baby. If you and the baby need a place to stay, you got one. But I ain't taking care of no grown man," Ouida had told her when Nola first found out about the baby. Nola had listened to her mother with tears in her eyes.

"Well, he's gonna have to find a way to make his feet walk over here. Your mama's got a few things to say to him and she's not wrong for wanting to say them. Is he going to Crescent?"

"Don't know. He didn't like the idea of going in that coal mine at all."

"No, the only idea he liked was the one got your belly stretched."

"El's not afraid of work. He say going in the mine is like being buried in a grave when you still living. He watched his daddy die from working in the mine, breathing that coal dust, breathing that death inside his chest every day."

"I ain't saying he's scared of work. But I know it's gonna take more than what he makes sitting on the lake waiting on fish to come to take care of a family."

"He don't have to take care of me. I'm gonna be working too, soon as the baby's big enough for me to have somebody watch."

"You two talk about all this?"

"We don't have to talk about it, that's just how it's gonna be."

"Well, all I know is you better get El to get them old long lanky legs over here and talk to your mama."

"She's not gonna talk, she's gonna scream. She's not gonna listen to nuthin we have to say, she's only gonna be listening to the thoughts she got running around in her head."

"And you gonna be the same way. You watch."

I I

N OLA MOVED SLOWLY through the house, dusting shelves and polishing glass. She listened to the muttering of her mother and her aunt as if listening to people whispering in a dream. She hadn't seen El in a week, and something inside the ground of herself shifted.

She was having trouble believing things were gonna be all right for her and the baby and El. "Sometimes believing is all you got," Bess had told Nola as she held her whimpering niece.

The baby had kicked inside Nola's belly two days ago. Before too long, it would be time. She knew her mother would not change her mind about El, not with this baby growing inside her.

Nola was afraid to have the baby, afraid to push the growing seed from the safety of her body into the chill of the awaiting world. Her mother's cruelty would be nothing compared to the rancor of the skinny-minded people of Pearl.

"You'd think they'd never seen a girl have a baby before, the way they blink their eyes and carry on," she mumbled. "Just like mama. Walking around the house with her mouth poked out. I know how she came up with me to take care of. She ain't the holy woman she thinks she is."

Nola stopped fussing when she came to the tarnished gold-plated frame holding their one picture of her father. She didn't look anything like him. He was a round-headed, yellow-skinned man with big crackling black eyes.

"They were the first thing I saw on him," her mother would sometimes say, laughing. "Big shiny fisheyes. That's what I thought when I first saw him. And he was all eyes, seeing and wondering about everything in the world."

Her mother didn't talk about him much around Nola or anybody else. She always said he was a piece of her life best forgotten unless she wanted to end up like Miss Buchanan and spend most of her time digging in the dump or out at the grave-yard, messing with dead folks' dreams.

Nola could not remember the sound of her father's voice, but she could recall the touch of his fingers brushing her cheeks. That touch, that one simple gesture belonging only to him, let her know how much he loved her. She longed for the gentleness that was his, now.

She quickly replaced the frame on the short table where it sat, an altarpiece. Raised voices in the kitchen made her hold herself still.

"Your hands are bloody as anybody's, Ouida. Only yours are more bloody cause you're supposed to be her mama," Nola heard Bess say.

"You're out of your mind."

"No, you've been out of your mind and I'm sick of it. That girl needs you now. You can't use them no more, so you wanna act like the wronged mama, when you're the one who's wrong."

"Just cause you got that liquor in you, you think you can talk to me any way you want? You must be out of your mind. This is my house and if you don't like what I say in my house, then I'll tell you the same thing I told that girl, GET OUT!" Nola's mother shouted.

"Running her away ain't gonna change the fact you're wrong and neither is running me off. In fact, that's exactly what you don't need, time to sit around here and think everything you've done in life is right, and we're all wrong. Well, you're wrong and I'm gonna keep on telling you you're wrong till you do right by that girl in there, who's carrying a baby. Your grandchild."

"I know I raised her right. I know I raised her better than to lay up with some fool that ain't got nuthin in his future but catching some fish. "

"This ain't got nuthin to do with how you raised her. She just about raised now and it's gonna be her turn soon to do the raising. Can't you see that? This is what she wanted. It didn't have nuthin to do with you."

"She mine, ain't she? What you mean it don't have nuthin to do with me? Who looked after her all these years after her daddy got hisself killed?"

"The man's dead and gone. Don't bring him up in this conversation."

"He was her daddy and my husband. I'll bring him up, turn him over, dance with him round the room if I want to."

"Ouida, what good is this? How's it gonna help anybody? You can't let that man rest after eight years?"

"If you settled down and stayed away from them whiskey bottles long enough to find you a man and get married, you could see what all this is about. If that man had stayed home instead of running behind that woman, I never would've had to shoot him and Nola would still have a father . . . "

"You didn't own that man, Ouida. You don't own Nola and you don't own me. If Sanford wanted to run behind a hundred women, you couldn't have stopped him, no matter what you did. You know why? Cause you can love them but you can't own them. Don't nobody own nobody else. And for you to sit up in here all these years shriveling up and trying to put your bitterness off on Nola is wrong. She has the right to try to make a life for herself the best way she knows how, just like you did. Didn't nobody tell you to run all the way from Jackson, Mississippi to Pearl, Washington to marry that man. And didn't nobody tell me to come out here with you. I came so you wouldn't be here without no people. That was something you had to do, and I had to do, like Nola's gonna do what she has to. The difference is, she don't have to get cut out of your life like mama cut you out of hers."

"You see all I gave up for him? You see?"

"All I see is a woman who's done tasted some bitter water, and didn't nobody tell her to go to the well and drink. You took a long enough swallow and now the bitterness left you so you thirsty still. And I don't need to live with no man to know that."

Nola turned and walked back to her room. She didn't want the women to know she had been listening to their angry exchange. For the last few months she had noticed the distance growing between her mother and her aunt. The rift between them was almost as great as the one between her mother and herself. Her mother's sharp glances, deep sighs and wringing hands had all been signs of her growing discontent. And for all of her mother's suppressed and expressed rage against her for the crime of her pregnancy, Bess had given her an equal dose of hugs, back rubs and foot massages. She saw her mother's resentment bubbling like a blister festering on a lip.

Soon Bess strode angrily through Nola's bedroom into her back room and slammed the door. Nola could hear her grumbling as she rustled through her drawers. A loud thump on the floor, and Nola knew she was packing the blue flowered suitcase she kept in her closet.

Before Nola could decide whether to go and soothe her aunt, her mother marched into the room.

"She in there?"

Nola nodded while her mother faced Bess's closed door as if she were preparing to knock it from its hinges.

"And what you mean I've got blood on my hands?"

"You know what I mean."

"You open this door and talk to me. We're gonna settle this once and for all."

"Not in front of Nola, we're not. What I got to say is for your ears alone, and you know what I'm gonna say."

"If you got anything that makes sense to say, you better say it now, Bess."

"Ouida, get away from my door."

"This is my door, in my house."

"I see you wanna keep reminding me of that."

"Well, it seems like you keep forgetting that one important fact. This is my house, it ain't no flophouse for liquored-up women."

"Here it comes. You really ready for this, Ouida? You sure this is what you want?"

"I ain't got a thing to hide, Bessie Yarbro. And you know it!"

"Nola, you take a little walk up the road for a spell. I'll come looking for you when me and your mama done spoke our piece," Bess said to Nola.

"Nola is mine," Ouida stated. "She's my daughter and don't nobody tell her what to do but me. You go lay up with some man and let him lie to you about how he love you and then get his baby and watch him act a fool behind some lowlifed witch. Then you watch him walk out the door and leave you and your baby. When that happens to you, then you can come around here and try to tell somebody else what to do."

Bess slowly opened the door. Her eyes looked as if they could fly out of her face. Nola didn't look at her mother when she left the room. Ouida slammed the bedroom door behind her daughter. As Nola moved toward the front door, she heard stillness in a voice usually filled with laughter and love.

"You watched them," she heard Bess say.

"What?"

"You watched Nola and that boy."

"You lying," her mother said.

"No, Ouida. And you know I'm not lying, don't you?"

"You must be out of your mind with liquor."

"No, you must be out of your mind," Bess said. "You watched your own daughter lay down and get a baby and you knew it was going to happen and you didn't tell her a thing, did you?"

"What I got to tell her?"

"You got plenty to tell her, Ouida. You got to tell her what happened to you and mama when y'all got pregnant. You got to tell her about life and loving. You got to tell her how you stood up in them trees at night and watched her kiss and hug on that boy you claim to hate so. You got to tell her what happened to Sanford. You at least got to tell her that, cause she has a right to know."

"She knows I didn't raise her . . . "

"You didn't raise her to be scared of loving nobody, thank God. But that ain't what you're mad about. You're mad because it ain't you."

"I know you done lost your mind now," her mother said.

"You're mad cause didn't El or nobody else lay you down out in them trees . . . "

"I don't have to listen to this."

"You're wrong, Ouida. You do have to listen to this, cause I'm the only one around here who's got the nerve to tell you about yourself. And I saw you. I saw how you'd look at that boy when he came around here for Nola. How you'd try to brush up against him when you thought nobody was looking. How you'd shrink up when he'd grab hold of her hand. But I told you a long time ago, it wasn't natural what you was doing. It wasn't right how you shot Sanford and got away with it, but you did. Then after you'd done all the mourning anybody'd ever have to do, and it was time for you to open yourself to life again, you didn't. You wanted to hang on to the memory of that man like it was a worry bead, rolling the same old thoughts around in your hands till it made you sick."

Nola didn't know if she wanted to hear any more, but she couldn't make herself open the door and leave the house. She'd never heard her aunt talk to her mother like this. She heard a scuffling sound.

"Don't let another one of your filthy lies out of your mouth in my house!" Nola heard her mother yell.

Nola moved quickly to the closed door. She heard the heavy breathing of the two sisters.

"Take your hands off me! I'm not going to be quiet till you hear all I got to say. And you can believe me, when I'm done saying what I got to say, you won't ever have to worry about me doing or saying anything else in your house again."

"Get out!" Her mother yelled again.

"Don't you worry about that. I'm gonna lay something else on your mind. Something you really need to be worried about. Cause I saw you. I saw you go out and stand up in the dark next to them trees. I could see the sweat on your face from where I was looking out the window, wondering if you had truly lost your mind at last. I watched you rub all up in your dress. Oh, yeah, I saw it all, Ouida. You wouldn't have to have nuthin but common sense to see what was going on in your mind. Even stone drunk, I know what it looks like when somebody wants somebody. And I know the way they want them. Like you wanted El. You wanted to be the one he was laying on and sweating over down in that grass. In your sick mind, it was your lips he should've been kissing, not Nola's."

"She don't know what to do with no man."

"But El ain't nuthin but a boy, Ouida. He ain't no man yet. Why don't you stay out of it and leave them both alone. You had your chance, let them have theirs."

"No," her mother said.

"What?"

"I said no. Don't neither one of them know what they want. How they gonna know? Nola hasn't even been out of Pearl."

"You been out, what good it do you? You a grown woman sneaking around peeking on two kids loving, wishing it was you."

"You don't know nuthin about my wishes. You don't know nuthin. Not a thing," her mother said.

"I saw you, Ouida. I saw you standing up in them trees touching yourself. And don't forget, I *have* been out of Pearl."

"Long enough to start sucking on that bottle."

"I'd rather suck on a bottle than snatch a boy from the cradle," Bess said.

"You get out of my house. GET OUT OF MY HOUSE!"

"Oh, I'm gonna get out of your house all right. But that don't mean the truth I'm telling's gonna leave too. No matter where I go or how far, what I'm saying is still gonna be true."

I I I

▼

NOLA HEARD THE DOOR CLOSE to the room that used to be Bess's. She sat down hard on the worn wooden planks of the front porch. She looked up. The sky pushed its silver upon the trees surrounding the house. Fistlike, the sun's red face struck from behind a thicket of clouds. The heat of its rays slashed her body. The wind blew the red dust in the yard until it gathered and rolled down the road like bloodstones. Ari crowed from the back of the house. Nola couldn't feel herself breathing, couldn't feel the drumbeat of her heart.

Ouida Barnett moved stiffly through the front door. She flicked her eyes quickly over Nola's face. She knew her daughter had heard every one of Bess's nasty words. Ouida looked like the air had been let out of her, but she still moved with the dignity and strength of an ages-old rage. Her eyes didn't see the heavy gray of the pressing sky, the bloody look of the sun or the angry whispering of the wind. She fixed her eyes on the memory of the naked corpse of her dead husband, the limp flesh between his legs, the one clean hole in his chest. Years ago, she had watched the other woman's house and waited. Waited till Sanford was alone in there. He had walked away from his wife and child, walked straight down the road to lie in that woman's bed.

He hadn't even opened his eyes when Ouida stood in the bedroom, gun in hand. He had looked so content in that bed, so sweet.

That's how he needs to go out of this world, she'd thought as she pulled the trigger. Satisfied as the day he was born.

Now the memory of his caresses had gotten tangled up with his lies, so now the only pure, undiluted picture of him she could call to mind was that one—where he lay with his mouth closed, his fleshy lips, which could only tell the truth now, sealed. As she looked at that picture now, she opened those crackling black fisheyes and fixed them with the hatred in her own.

"Look what you done turned me into," was all Nola heard her mother say as she stiffly brushed past Nola and moved out into the wind, beneath the demanding sky. The sun touched her with its bloody fingers, and Nola saw Ouida tremble but keep moving across the yard and onto the road.

"Mama!" Nola called into the listening wind. "Mama, where you going?"

Ouida Barnett did not turn her head; she held her body in its odd, stiff pose and moved with only a single thought in her mind.

"Where does she think she's going in all this wind?" Bess asked quietly as she stood behind Nola on the porch.

"She didn't say. I better go get her," Nola said, slowly rising to her feet.

"No, she needs to go wherever she's going, and she needs to get there by herself."

Nola watched the curious question that was her mother walk farther down the road, then into the trees. Nola turned to Bess.

"I heard what you said in there."

"I didn't want you to, but I guess it's something you was gonna find out one way or another," Bess said, gently stroking Nola's face.

"She always said a crazy woman shot my daddy."

"A crazy woman did, child," Bess said softly.

"Did she really watch us, me and El, I mean?"

"Yeah, she really did."

"But why, why would she do something like that?"

"That's something you're gonna have to ask her. I don't have no answers for you, all I got is questions myself."

"You ain't really leaving here, are you?" Nola asked.

"Soon as I can get to the depot in the morning."

"But what's gonna happen to Mama? Who she gonna have?"

Bess looked out at the sky and the rolling red dirt for a long time. Then she looked into Nola's weary eyes.

"I guess she's gonna have who she's always had," she said after a while, then turned and walked into the house.

The sky moved its silver from the trees, the sun went back behind the clouds and the wind stopped its shivery whispering. Nola sat on the porch and thought about what her aunt and mother had said. Did her mother shoot her father? Had her mother really seen her and El in the woods?

Nola shivered when she recalled the chilly fingers of the wind caressing their naked flesh, the easy way she had opened. She could not believe her mother had seen all that. But Bess had said her mother wanted El, wanted El like Nola herself wanted him. She could not imagine her mother opening herself and eager, could not see that old braced woman damp with the moisture of desire.

A battered black Buick roared down the road and stopped in front of her mother's house. Little Dupree was at the wheel, crying.

"Something's happened to El!" he shouted.

"What?" Nola jumped from the porch and ran to the car.

"El gone. Nick Adams was out in the woods and found him laying in a hole, not moving, not breathing, not nuthin. He did away with hisself, like the old ones did. Found what we thought was bits of shiny marble in the hole. Turned out to be castor beans spread round his body. And you know they ain't nuthin but poison. You better get over to his mama's house quick!" was all he said before taking off down the road, leaving Nola standing at the side of the road like a stunned tree.

Bess came out of the house, saw Nola frozen by the road and ran to her.

"What's the matter, honey? What is it?"

Nola couldn't speak.

"Nola, Nola! What in the world's happened?" Bess said as she gathered Nola into her arms and held her as gently as she dropped sweet peas into the basket of her skirt.

"Is it your mama?"

Nola shook her head, opened her mouth and let the sound fall from her lips like a death rattle. "El," was all she said before falling to the ground.

I V

▼

A S SHE STEPPED FROM THE TRAIN, the sharp tang of Pearl's air sweetened her nostrils. Nola felt the same sadness she had felt when she left the town twelve years ago. She looked at the people milling on the platform, the same slow grace punctuating their movements. She knew the mountain, the trees and the lake would have all remained the same.

Miss Marius wasn't here yet with her daughter, Septeema. Even though she'd always let Miss Marius know where she stayed in Chicago, she'd set matches to the letters Miss Marius had sent to tell Nola of the growth of her daughter. Nola had set the matches and watched the letters burn, as she wanted her memories of Pearl to burn.

But hard as she tried to forget Pearl, Pearl had planted its roots into the fertile soil of her life. No matter how far or hard she ran from its memories and sadness, she knew now, she would always be a daughter of this town.

* * *

Nola moved past the drinking fountain and sat on a green wooden bench. The slats on its back were hard and she was uncomfortable, though she believed she deserved to be punished for leaving her daughter. But she hoped that returning to Pearl and reclaiming her daughter, as her own mother had never reclaimed her, would somehow make amends for her leaving.

El had never forgiven himself, or her for leaving their daughter. She'd seen him staring at her in shiny fixtures and chrome bumpers, his sad eyes on her in store windows and mirrors. Especially mirrors. It had gotten so she couldn't even look into glass without El standing up behind her asking about his baby girl.

And Nola had cursed him, "You left her too, El!" she'd cry. She also cursed her mama, Aunt Bess and the baby, Miss Marius and any kind of god she could call on. She had cursed them all till she looked at her own bloody hands and cursed herself.

Even now, she winced from the memory of the sting of the camphor, okra, and berries she had mashed and put between her legs to bring the baby out. And after all that burning, the baby had come anyway, alive and whole.

Then her mother had gotten so she couldn't look Nola in the face, took to slipping to the woods at night, talking to the trees. Her mother spent hours wandering through the graveyard and moaning so until some folks believed the Night People had snatched her soul.

Nola had decided to leave then, leave the baby and Bess, her crazy mama and El. She decided to leave them all in Pearl. Nola wrote Bess shortly after she got to Chicago, so someone in the world would know where she was.

Bess stayed a while longer in Pearl and tried to help Ouida with the baby as long as she could. But Bess had always said there wasn't never going to be a mother inside her, so she cut her ties to Ouida Barnett and moved back home to Jackson. Before she left, she passed Nola's address to Miss Marius.

Miss Marius had taken the baby into her house, since Ouida Barnett was barely able to take care of herself, let alone an unwanted child.

El gone, Bess gone. Her mama never really there. Miss Marius had sent a note when her mama passed. Nola hadn't come for the burial. Her mama had been dead to her the day they found El buried in a shallow grave in the woods and her mother had gone down the road in a red wind.

SECTION 3

Things Handed Down

I

Sin-Sin

▼

S IN-SIN SAT ON THE DEPOT PLATFORM looking at the sparkly dark woman who drifted like a vision from the train.

The way she stood gazing at the town made Sin-Sin think about his dream from the night before. The flat open look in her eye, the way she stood trembly in the pointy-toed shoes, and the soft orange mist floating around her face like gray that had trickled from an old faded picture and come to life, all made him think about the dream. But it was the funny orange mist that made him think about his daddy. And Sin-Sin only saw his daddy in his dreams.

Sin-Sin turned his eyes from the woman waiting, pulled his mind from the things his daddy had told him in the dream last night. He didn't have time to think about them now. Blue was waiting. Waiting for him out in the woods.

"What you got in your hand, boy?"

Sin-Sin turned his head toward the scratchy voice calling him. He gripped the small brown package tight with his armpit and made his body hard, like Blue had told him to do: "Harder, harder. So can't nobody get inside your soul."

"Where you off to in such a hurry?"

Sin-Sin looked at fat-eyed Roy. He didn't say nuthin. Blue had told him not to.

"Left your tongue out in them woods, boy? I know your mama taught you to speak to folk when they speaking to you."

"Nowhere, Mr. Roy. I ain't going nowhere."

"Well, what your hurry, then? You can sit awhile and talk to an old man, can't you?"

"No, sir. Got to be on my way. Got somebody waiting on me."

"Who?"

"My mama."

"Oh. Well. You can't keep your mama waiting, can you?"

"No sir."

"Well, we'll sit and visit some other time, then. Some time when you ain't so busy. I got some questions to ask about that man stays out in the woods. Guess you about the only one can tell me what I want to know, since you out in them woods about as much as he is."

Sin-Sin hated to lie to Roy about going to meet his mama, but he didn't want to answer any of his questions about Blue. Too many folks in town had questions about Blue, things they didn't want to ask him themselves, but were always trying to get back-way answers through Sin-Sin.

"I don't know if I can tell you much, Mr. Roy. You better ask Blue any questions you got," Sin-Sin said as he started running down the street.

"You better watch out for that man, Sin-Sin. You don't know

what-all he can do!" Roy shouted after Sin-Sin's retreating frame.

Sin-Sin ran through the middle of town kicking up red dust. He ran past the general store where his mama bought the food that didn't grow in their yard or some neighbor's, past Reverend Daniles's one-room insurance office where the minister stayed when he wasn't working in the church. "All my work's about insurance," Reverend Daniles always said, laughing his big-bellied laugh.

Sin-Sin ran on, out past the One Eye Cafe where men from the east side of town gathered for liquid communion.

He did not slow his steps until he could no longer hear the cawing laughter of the men inside the Cafe. He loosened the grip of his arm on the small brown bag and gasped when it fell to the ground and tore open.

Inside a thin white bed of tissue lay a knife, made out of black wood. A crocodile was carved into the bow of the knife, complete with protruding eyes, a jagged-toothed mouth, and waves of scales on its bottom. Sin-Sin had watched Blue shape this very knife out in the woods; now he held its sharp sleekness to his cheek. The scales felt like water rolling over his skin.

"When it's your time, boy, you'll have your own knife."

"My mama says I don't need to be messing around with no knives."

"This ain't got nuthin to do with your mama," Blue had told him without blinking.

"But if she finds out . . . "

"Naw, your time ain't noways near. You still worrying behind what your mama tell you to say and do. I must've had you figured wrong. Got you mixed up with somebody ready."

"I'm ready. I'm ready. I just don't . . . "

"You just don't what?"

"I just don't know, that's all. How's my mama gonna even know I'm a man when I come back if she don't know what's going on?"

"She'll know."

"But how?"

"Some things you see and some you say. There's plenty of ways to come to a knowing besides clacking your teeth."

Blue had sent him the sign like he said he would.

Sin-Sin tapped the knife against a fingertip. A bright dot of blood pooled. He sniffed the blood, then licked his finger. He wondered if his blood would be different, turned into some new kind of water, after he became a man.

I I

▼

FAR OFF DOWN THE ROAD, two dots moved in Sin-Sin's direction. The dots moved slow, like his daddy did when he was coming into Sin-Sin's dreams.

The first dream had scared him. He was seven years old and finally able to fall asleep without his mother lying beside him on the bed. He had slid into his dreaming for the night, easily.

Then he was falling. Falling slowly, slowly into a wide crack in the center of the world, his orange body floating through soft black light.

When his body hit the bottom of the hole there in the middle of the earth, he lay still, listening.

He felt footsteps on the ground, steps dragging toward him, rolling across the earth like tongues moving over skin.

He saw a winter circle of eyes, mute yellow eyes, circling round his body like old fading stars.

An orange mist rose from the ground, and as Sin-Sin sank his fingers into the mist's moistness, he watched his fingers disappear.

The mist wrapped itself around his body until he felt comforted and warm. He believed nothing could hurt him while he was enclosed in the soft glowing mist.

Sin-Sin had not dreamed of the mist again until last night.

He was in a green place, a deep emerald place in the woods near Blue's. The trees there were bare-bottomed and tall, the flowering branches near the tops were black arms covered with soft leafy fur. The air was moist, the sky a green so alive it sang. Its soft murmuring song began to lull Sin-Sin to sleep at the bottom of a witch tree.

Sin-Sin knew he had sat beneath a witch tree because one time Blue had drawn a picture of the tree in the dirt with a stick. The trunk was almost as tall as Sin-Sin. A ball of curled-up limbs sat at the top of the tree.

Blue told him the Night People lived inside the thick, heavy branches that curled around themselves like a mass of wooden snakes.

"But I thought the Night People was tall. How can they live all squished up inside them twisted-up branches?"

"You ever seen a snake stretch out from a coil? She might look little when she's all curled around, but when she loosens up and pulls out, she's a mighty long, serious line."

The drawing had scared Sin-Sin. Made him feel small.

"The Old Ones like these trees cause they look like them. See how the tree has them skinny branches growing out of the thick ones, hanging down like hair? When you see an Old One, one of the Night People, you tell me what she looks like."

* * *

Blue had shaken his head and laughed to himself. "Once you see one of them, you know what power is, boy. They able to reach inside you, so you can call up the words that let you know your name."

Sin-Sin didn't care if he never saw one of the trees cause Blue's scratching in the ground looked a bit too powerful to him. He didn't want Blue to see it, though, the folding-in feeling in his eyes.

Now, in his dream, Sin-Sin sat at the foot of this great strange tree, almost asleep. He smiled, remembering his fear. The sky's green song was gentle, the tree's bark soft as fur. His closed eyes twitched sporadically, then were still. Soon, out on the edge of dream he felt a presence, some old cold thing drawing near. He tried to open his eyes, but couldn't. He felt the coldness moving toward him until it stood around him solid as ice. He stretched out an arm as if to ward off a blow. He heard what he thought was one continuous sound, but when he felt the air blowing from the old thing's lips, he heard a chant, a multitude of voices mumbling a whistling chant. He could not make out the words, but there was a heavy sadness in the air now. The sadness moved over his body until he felt the weight of a thousand years of sorrow stirring inside his young thin bones.

The tree's naked branches rubbed against themselves as if touching would clothe them and take the heavy sadness out of the air. The branches moved closer to Sin-Sin until he felt their icy touch deep within his dream.

He shivered and tried once more to open his eyes. The branches fell softly around his body and reached beneath his shrinking form to lift him into the air.

At last he could open his eyes. The misty air was orange here, at the top, above the other trees. He lay within the black cup of branches. He looked as the thick air pressed him deeper inside the tree until he felt its sap moving like blood around his bones.

He pushed his eyes open, far as he could, then touched his face with trembly fingers.

The mist moved with a slow orange grace over his body, stroking him, calming his tremors. The air smelled like wet rock and its salt left damp silver streaks across his skin. He was not afraid. He was up so high no one would find him here.

The slow-moving mist began to hum with a low sound, an old moan from deep inside somebody's bones. The moan moved from a deep place out of the sky into Sin-Sin's own blood and bones. He twisted inside the black cup of branches with his eyes wide open. There was someone standing there, just beyond the edge of his senses, someone he had known before, waiting for the right moment to step inside his dream.

I I I

▼

OFTEN SIN-SIN REMEMBERED the first time he had ever talked to
Blue.

"What's the word, boy?"

"Huh?"

"I said what's the word?"

"What word?"

"I thought you somebody I been waiting on."

"Ain't nobody waiting on me, except maybe my mama."

"Oh, that's how it is."

"How what is?"

"How you find your way back out here, don't none of them
schoolboys come out around here, you ain't scared of these
woods?"

"Ain't nuthin out here to be scairt of I know about."

"Then that shows how much you know."

"Huh?"

"Plenty out here to be scairt of, you got the sense to be."

"To be what? Scairt?"

"Yourself."

"Why you talking like that?"

"How else I'm supposed to talk? Like your mama?"

"You know my mama?"

"All I need to know is right here in my hand. Let me see one of yours."

"They kind of dirty."

"There's all kind of schools, boy, this one it don't matter what's on the shell, it's the meat inside that count."

"Huh?"

"You'll do. Once you close your mouth and stop asking other folks' questions, you'll be all right."

Blue had dropped his hand and walked off deeper into the woods. Sin-Sin didn't know what to think of Blue or his funny talk, but he did know Blue was the only living soul besides his mama who'd ever told him he was gonna be all right, and Blue was the only one who even knew that question was in Sin-Sin's mind.

I V

OFTEN, BLUE AND SIN-SIN MET at a cleared-off spot in a circle of
white pines. Blue did most of the talking, while Sin-Sin listened and tried to understand.

"What you know about time, boy?"

"I know how to tell it."

"I'm not talking about telling time, I'm talking about knowing time. How it feels when you hold it in your hand, rub it up
against your lips."

"I've held a clock in my hands, but I didn't never want to kiss it."

"Just what I thought."

"What?"

"Nuthin."

"What?"

"You don't know nuthin about time. You can't tie time up in
no kind of machine and look, it's something alive and moving,

always. All around us. You think these trees look at a clock to know where they at and when the light's gonna come and the whys of things?"

"But that's how we tell it at my house."

"That ain't telling nuthin, boy. Time ain't for telling, it's for knowing. And the knowing is inside you and all around. That's how these trees know more about this world than you, cause they know what time is, by living it."

"Trees don't know nuthin about the world, they can't even talk."

"Talking don't mean you know nuthin, like I told you before. You talking now, but you don't know what you talking about. These trees were here before anybody you know, and lots you don't. So how you gonna say they don't know nuthin? They been here since near the beginning, boy. Don't you never forget about that."

Sin-Sin would sometimes shrink inside himself after talking with Blue. Blue always made him think about things he never would've thought about himself, and it seemed like whatever he said was the wrong thing to say to Blue.

His answers to Blue's strange questions were the same as any other boy's would be, he thought. But once when he voiced this opinion to Blue, Blue's short response had chilled him.

"Ain't nuthin about you like them other boys."

It was the thing Sin-Sin was most afraid of. He was different and everybody knew. Everybody knew he was different and didn't fit, like some crazy-edged piece in a smooth-sided puzzle.

He tried not to say things that would make him stand out, tried to fade into the background at school, never talked out of turn in class. He made his eyes small when they felt big, laughed when Tad and those girls tried to make him cry at school.

"Mama's little baby loves shortnin', shortnin';
mama's little baby loves shortnin' bread . . . "

He often longed for darkness, for cover, for something soft and strong to keep the light from his face.

In the dark there would be no laughter ringing inside his head, no sharp eyes cutting his skin from the bone. In the dark there would be no big hands holding or small fingers reaching, there would be no screaming, no music, no sound. There would be no mothers without fathers, no children without names.

In the warmth of that black light, that dark cavernous space, he could lose himself, shed his skin like a bursting orange sun and stand naked within himself, bask in the dark light of himself, touch the deep shining hole inside himself and fill it, at last.

But now there was no such darkness, only the brilliant light that shines on those who stand out from the crowd. Sin-Sin knew unquestionably that that light was shining on him now for all to see, even Blue.

"Mama's little baby loves . . . "

He never should have told Raisin about the dream that day in the woods. He didn't remember the look on her face when he told her the story. He had felt as if he were talking inside an echoing bowl, some round dome over his head filled with water and the sound of his words going around and over and moving back again inside his mind without his lips moving, his dry wooden lips that would not sing.

". . . shortnin', shortnin'; Mama's little baby . . . "

It was the closest he had come to telling anyone who he thought his daddy was, but the truth could not be told easy, his mama had told him. The truth she had held inside herself dense as dream.

V

▼

Look at yourself, boy," Blue would say to Sin-Sin. "Read you like a book. How you gonna keep folks out of your soul?"

"What? What did I do?"

"You think you got something missing, don't you, boy?"

"Huh?"

"I can see it in the shape your body makes when you move through these trees. All slouched over and into yourself, like a big old empty fisheye in the middle of your chest. You think I'm the only one what sees it? The only one what know?"

"Know what?"

"About what you think is gone."

"I don't know what you mean."

"Sure you do, boy. Sure you do. Take your time and let your body feel and remember. It's still there, you the only one what thinks it's gone."

"What's gone? I don't think nuthin's gone."

"What about your daddy?"

"Don't got no daddy."

"Everybody gots a daddy, boy. Even you. Let me see your hand. I'm gonna rub some of the green from this leaf on it. There. See the way them lines come together in the middle? What kind of shape that look like to you?"

"Looks like a wide-open eye."

"It is a eye. You gotta eye right in the middle of your hand. The Old Ones say you got one of these, you got all kind of power. You can touch things and know them. You can put your hand to something broken and make it feel all right. You can see all kinds of things with that hand, boy. You sit yourself down and look on it for a while. Look in it and see, but don't use your eyes. Use what you got inside to see."

V I

▼

As Sin-Sin walked deeper into the black-green air, to the place where he was to meet Blue, he wondered if Blue knew about his dreams. It seemed like Blue knew what Sin-Sin was thinking before he knew himself. He stopped walking and inhaled deeply. This must be what it smelled like at the beginning of the world, he thought. The earthy aroma of some dark secret flower.

He looked at the sleek knife gleaming in the palm of his hand. Beneath the knife, his hand-eye watched without blinking.

"What you want to tell me now?" he asked gently, smiling.

It had taken him a while to learn how to look into that eye without feeling scared. And even longer still to trust his insides to see for him instead of his eyes.

"You want to know who your daddy is, just look in that eye and see. That old eye knows. That and a whole lot more. Your body remembers things you never thought you knew, stories you ain't been told. But you hold them there inside you like a second heart."

Blue was right. Without seeing, he could feel. Without knowing, he could remember what he didn't even know he knew.

Sin-Sin looked inside his hand, deep inside the eye there and felt his mother, Aimee Dubois.

She was young and slim then. She wore hope around her body like a brightly colored sash. She was a pale yellow woman, fragile as crumbling lace. A young woman running from the stifling mold of her own mother's life.

Unlike Sin-Sin, she knew her father. Knew his raging moods, the tears of failure shining in his eyes, the angry slit-eyed look from the women who laid beneath him hoping to patch some small piece of the emptiness they could see in his eyes, an emptiness enticing as narcotics. A woman whose emptiness was more vast than her father's had brought Aimee Dubois to her father's house for him and his stiff wife to raise.

Aimee Dubois had known cruelty before she could write her own name. The great crushing cruelty of the coward, the indifference and hypocrisy of a woman so devoted to her god, so fanatically Christian, she could forsake the living, especially the needy young girl living inside her home here on earth.

The woman treated Aimee like the stepchild she was and never let her husband or Aimee forget it.

Aimee clung to the belief that her father loved her, though he had never told her those magic words. She had to believe in his love, in somebody's love, because it was the only way she could endure the years of wifely rage directed at her, the illegitimate child her father had brought home, the filth and sin he had dared bring into his wife's heavenly home, and tainted with the stench of adultery.

But when her father had walked into a room in a cousin's

house and seen Aimee pinned to a bed by an older cousin, had seen the smallness of her young body squirming beneath the bulk of the cousin who was using her bones to excite himself, when her father walked in and saw and turned and left without saying a word, without a look or a gesture to frighten or stop the cousin, without any small comforting sound for Aimee, she knew and understood then that even her father did not love her and perhaps all the hateful words his wife had hurled at her were true: that she was a good-for-nothing like her whorish mother, and would end up just like her, unloved.

Once she knew her father did not love her, would not protect her or help her if she needed it, she decided she would leave New Orleans, get as far away from the sidelight of her father's stifling house as she could. In the meantime she would fill her head with words and sounds, escape into the worlds awaiting her inside books.

Aimee read and dreamed and filled her head with words on paper. She finished her schooling, became a schoolteacher and moved to Pearl without leaving a forwarding address.

She would reinvent herself, make herself into something she'd only read about, once she had settled in Pearl.

She didn't dream when she first came to Pearl. The stillness of the days followed her into the nights, and except for the children of the school and Reverend Daniles, she spoke to no one.

She filled the silence pooling within the walls of her four-room house by reading the Bible, scribbling poems about beauty and sitting in front of the cinnamon-colored bricks of the fireplace, singing into the fire.

Although she first attended services at Reverend Daniles's church, she soon grew tired of the steady eyes of the churchgoers boring into her back. She could feel their questions about her penetrating the severe cloth of her long dresses. She suspected they talked about her, as she was a newcomer to the town, that they could somehow sense her worthlessness. Soon she stopped subjecting herself to their scrutiny and began staying at home with the comfort of lines on paper and no mirrors in anyone's eyes.

She loved the stillness of Pearl, the green aura of its towering evergreens, the glow of the red dirt-covered double-headed mountain and the small body-blue hills running from the mountain's heads like a spine.

She did not feel as empty here as she had at home, and when she sat on the bank of the smooth black lake and cast her line into its secret waters, she felt as wondrous as a wave. This was where she had church now. She'd sit and listen to the sermons of the preaching birds and mosquitoes, the crackling old tree branches and the lilting selections from the wind, communion broken only when she pulled a struggling streak of silver from the water to take home and clean for her evening meal.

A few months after she arrived in Pearl, when the easy rhythm of moving from her bed to her car (the only car out on this side of town), to the school and the blank-eyed children, to her car again, back to her house and maybe through the trees to the lake and back to her bed again, when the easiness of this rhythm became almost enough to get her biting the knuckles of her fists, the air around her house began to change.

The air slowed its movement and then stopped. It laid over her house until it seemed like she was living inside a cup turned upside-down on a saucer.

Then one day when she stepped inside her house it was as if she were stepping into a soundless abyss without color or time. She felt a rush of water, a great body of water, moving inside her. Then as soon as she crossed the threshold, all movement stopped.

She forced herself to stretch her legs toward the kitchen, move her arms inside the room as she fixed herself food to eat. She had to have nourishment for her body, to keep up her strength for the flow of her days, the hollowness of moving from one small container into another, until her body filled with a silence so loud it echoed.

She pushed the bread into her mouth, felt the coarseness of its skin. Water rolled gently down her throat, soothing her with its coolness. She was sweating now, all the time sweating. She held the steaming dish of potatoes and cheese to her nose and filled her head with its vapor. She poured salt into her hands and licked her palms. Each brackish bead of salt filled her with a longing so deep, her eyes burned.

She began opening, all over the house opening: drawers, containers, boxes of books. She threw open the door to her bedroom and opened the window. It was hot. The heat made her sleepy. She laid on the bed and pulled the sheets to her body close as a lover. The only sound inside her head, a soft whimper. Even the air smelled of something opening, flesh unlocking from flesh.

Though it was light outside, soon, oh very soon, the shadows on the wall would be as black as she was, lying there, open in her bed, naked legs clinching the sheets as if she were riding them. She could not open her mouth now, even to pray for early darkness.

Soon she slept and dreamed she was an island. A long yellow broken piece of land floating in black water. A land uninhabited by man.

When she opened her eyes, the night's dark had fanned into her room.

A high moon cast a slash of white light on her bed. She heard the sound of something dragging around the house, some long thing circling. She was not afraid of the sound, not afraid when the dragging stopped outside her window.

An orange mist poured through the window as a man climbed into the room.

"You again?"

"I told you I'd be back."

"They're all going to think I've lost my mind."

"How are they going to know?"

"You know what can happen from this."

"You'll have someone who'll never leave you."

"You?"

"You."

"I'm going to have more than me if this turns out like I think it might."

"We all need something more than ourselves some times, as long as we know it for what it is."

"Like I know you?"

"I'm not your daddy."

"And you're not God, so why do I keep listening to you?"

"Cause you've got a need and I've got a need."

"How do you know about my needs?"

"I can smell you when you out in the woods."

"Well, it's been hot lately and I haven't been myself."

"You've been more yourself than you've ever been."

"They're going to build a crazy house just for me here, they find out about this."

"Nobody gonna find out. You ain't gonna tell nobody, not even the boy."

"What boy?"

"You'll see and you'll know and remember what I said. What you crying for?"

"What kind of life is this?"

"It's the one you signed up for, the one you agreed to live. You wanted all of this, your daddy, your mama, me, the boy. You wanted this. Don't you remember?"

"No. I don't know what you're talking about. You're not even real."

"I'm real as your life, Aimee. As real as the need shining between your legs."

The mist covered her body as the man stood next to her bed. She reached for the warmth of her breasts and held them up into the vapor, her nipples standing like hard bits of orange chocolate. She smelled the sea of herself, the sea of what she sensed inside the cloud around the man.

He pressed himself upon her body. She pushed her body against his. Her tongue became serpentine. Her body a rolling mass of flame.

Somewhere, deep inside, her unblemished core was touched and released.

She wanted to submerge and cleanse herself, obliterate then create herself, within the lush cloud and the man moving inside her.

A woman, Sin-Sin murmured, rubbing his knee with his hand-eye. The young wanting woman he had seen was his mother.

He marveled at the tenderness of the man who'd made her moan with pleasure, marveled at the ease with which the woman in his mother had blended with the body of the man.

He couldn't help but wonder now if that faceless man in the orange mist was Blue.

The Space Between Words Where People Live

I

Raisin

▼

DON'T KNOW HOW LONG them watery whispers crying, "Baby girl
... Baby girl," hold me fixed to that spot in the road. I see
Miss Marius walking, not paying me no attention, but I can't
even blink my eye.

When Miss Marius look like a speck on the road, the whispers let me go. My arms fall like branches cut from a tree and my
body start to move again.

I look all around me into the trees, but don't see nobody and
it don't seem like nobody see me. I'm glad. I don't know what
folks'd say if they saw me standing like that out on the road.

I cock my head and listen, but all I hear is the same woodsounds. Not one solitary whisper.

I pick my legs up cause I can, and run down the red road to
Miss Marius. The trees standing off from the road like stuck-up
women admiring theirselves are a green so dark they almost black.

I don't tell Miss Marius about the whispers cause I don't want her to tell this Nola woman I ain't got good sense. When she turn her head to look at me puffing up alongside her and shake her head, I'm glad that's all she do.

We both walk the rest of the way to town without saying nuthin. But I know we're both thinking about who's waiting at the train depot.

When we're almost at the depot, Miss Marius say, "I used to always dream about trains. Them long silvery tracks leading to some new kind of life and folks who don't know nuthin about you. I used to know the train's timetable like I know the wrinkles in my own body. Chicago. Detroit. Memphis. New York. For some reason I got the notion to see one of them big cities where buildings raise up out of the ground like strange steel flowers and folks rush past each other like they're running to catch their yesterdays, since tomorrows ain't promised to none of us.

"See, I thought I was too big for Pearl, these simple folks around here too dumb for me. I wanted to get out in the middle of that energy running around the world. Wanted to see and do things I didn't even understand, but I knew there was something important in the doing. Didn't want to sit and let no moss grow under my feet.

"Seem like that's one of the worst things in the world. Sitting up and waiting on something to happen instead of getting out there and grabbing hold of it with your own bare hands and shaking, shaking life for all it's worth.

"And instead of getting all twisted up and over, behind the suffering and hard times that will surely come your way, you learn how to smooth out the knotted spots inside yourself, making you think you're a piece of nuthin and everybody else is a piece of something bigger and better than you.

"There's something about a train track. Where it's all

smoothed-out and cold, and laid out sure as you please running cross rivers and mountains, and out where the land is flat and endless as everything there ever was and will be.

"I used to stand in the middle of the track when I heard a train coming in. Stand right in the middle and look it in the eye. That's what life is, Raisin. A big old hard-smooth piece of steel coming that you've got to look dead in the eye. And whichever train come with your name on it, whichever one that come, you got to ride."

Miss Marius had said all she had to say by the time we reached the depot. She stopped walking when we reached the platform, so I stopped too. There's only one dark woman waiting at the drop-off. One dark woman say she my mama.

I look at that coat she got on. Coal-black fur look like something from a picture show. And her shoes! Tall black high-high heels. Don't nobody in Pearl have no shoes like them. And her legs silky shiny.

I look at Miss Nola Barnett's face. She don't look like nobody's mama to me. She got wood-black skin that smooth and shiny, and lips look like they ready to laugh. I can't see her eyes behind them glasses with pearls at the tips, only see me staring in the glass.

I don't look nuthin like this woman. She gonna know now she couldn't never be my mama. She pretty.

I stand behind Miss Marius and feel like I'm wrinkling even more. Woman like her wouldn't want no girlchild like me.

Miss Marius was looking at her kind of funny, but Miss Nola Barnett stared Miss Marius straight in her face, not shamed or nuthin.

"I guess you think you'll be taking her now," Miss Marius say. "Just like all these years don't mean nuthin to me or her?"

Miss Nola look at Miss Marius and pulled herself up in her picturehouse coat and say,

"Yes, ma'am. I mean no, ma'am. I mean I do expect to take her. She's mine. And I do know what it means to both of you and I'm here to show you how grateful I am."

They was looking at and talking to each other like I'm a speck of dust, or something they can't see floating around in the air. But I know her voice. She and that man voice calling me on the road.

"They don't make no pens or paper in Chicago?" Miss Marius ask.

"Yes, ma'am. They make them."

"We supposed to think anything but what we thought?"

"No. I mean yes," Miss Nola Barnett say.

"What?" Miss Marius ask.

For a minute, Miss Nola Barnett look small in her big shoes and fur coat. She take the pearly glasses off, but she still don't say nuthin.

Then finally, in a voice so small I wondered how it could've come out of a big fancy woman's body, how that voice could've sounded so strong before, Miss Nola Barnett say, "I paid with more than blood, Miss Marius. I paid with more than blood."

Miss Marius keep looking at Miss Nola till she satisfied with what she see.

I feel Miss Marius softening, start leaning toward Miss Nola. Her back ain't held quite so high. Miss Nola start to smile a bit round the corners of her mouth and next thing happen they pulling on each other so hard, it's a surprise they don't twist and fall down.

Ain't nuthin about Miss Nola Barnett familiar, cept that voice. I know I heard her talking before. She got a voice sound like water easing into water. A soft liquid sound. She still don't say nuthin to me. When they let go, both they faces wet. They keep holding and touching each other. Then they turn around to me.

I don't say nuthin, just look at the dust on my flat dress shoes. My socks are dusty and the bottoms of my legs look rusty. Even my good dress hanging on my body like a piece of sorry cloth.

What she see looking at me?

A speck of dust. An old wrinkled raisin. A piece of nuthin.

She don't say nuthin for so long I finally raise my head. Her eyes the black in dreams. I see things in em. Stars, cracked moons, an old dying sun.

I close my eyes cause she looking inside me. I can feel her looking right inside. Don't nobody look at me like that. Nobody in this world. I hold my body still cause this new. I wanna wiggle but don't want her to think I'm dumb.

Then I remember. Her voice. I must've heard it way before today, way way back when I was floating in her stomach. And I think about how long it took, but she did decide to give me life. She told Miss Marius to give me life.

"I know you don't remember me, Septeema," Miss Nola Barnett say. "I left here a long time ago. But I'm back now and I'm gonna be your mama till the day you die. This is for you."

She got a silver oval in her hand. Holding it out to me. To me. She brought something for me and she don't even know me yet. She don't see my skin. The wrinkles in my skin. I take the oval and hold it in my hand. I feel Miss Marius nodding but I don't look at her. The silver on the oval is old and not polished. I feel. Its rough skin feel just like mine. Feel like a big old round circle of a tree with branches hanging down to the ground. No. It feel like the big round fan on a peacock's behind.

A little button on the side. I push and the oval spring open. I jump cause I think I'm gonna drop it, drop it on the dusty ground before I get a chance to see inside. Then I jump again. I'm looking at me in my hand. Me and that blue blanket of a sky behind my head. Me, Septeema.

I don't know what to say. I don't like looking in no mirrors. Used to think I'd see a different me, but it's always the same me. So I leave em alone. Run from em sometime. Lucille like to catch me and hold me down and make me look. She think she gonna make me cry. But I don't. I look in that glass and pretend it's water. A big silver drop of water and I'm a fish swimming on through.

On the back side of the oval is a big black pearl. In the middle of the tail feather and all round the edge is red and green stones that catch and hold light.

I ain't never had nuthin like this.

Not no real mama, and not no real necklace, or rings for my ears, or nuthin.

Lucille say ain't nuthin gonna make me shine. But I look at the oval and the woman standing smiling, saying she my mama, MINE, and I know I don't never have to listen to what Lucille say no more. I look up at Miss Nola Barnett, look her dead in her eye and say, "Thank you, ma'am."

She lean into me but she don't touch and she say my name over and over like a question ain't no answer for, "Septeema?"

I don't answer cause I don't know no words for this feeling, or this woman say she my mama. But Miss Marius grab hold of one of my arms and Miss Nola Barnett grab the other and they pull me into they circle, and I hold my mirror so tight in my hand it leave marks.

I I

▼

WE WALK INSIDE THE DEPOT and wait for Miss Nola's bags.
Nathan coming around with his pickup truck to get them
after while. I see questions in the ticket-taker's ice-blue eyes, but
Miss Nola don't say nuthin to him.

"Some things the same the world over," was all she say. Miss
Marius just shake her head.

We stand in front of the depot to wait for Nathan. Miss Marius and Miss Nola keep talking and laughing. Miss Nola sound
like a car trying to start when she laugh.

I don't listen, just look. She can't go far in them shoes. Her fat
brown legs don't even wobble. Where she been to walk like that in
them shoes? Bet she won't even make it out of town. Look like she
walking on knives. I ain't gonna worry about it, though. Every once
in a while she stop talking and turn around. Look at me, wrinkle her
nose and smile. Miss Marius stop and look too, but she don't smile.

Nathan finally come and load up the truck with Miss Nola's things. Miss Marius gonna ride with him, me and Miss Nola gonna walk.

"Give us some time to make our acquaintance," she say, and I feel something tight close up inside.

"Now, let's see. The cemetery's out that way, right?"

I nod my head and hope this lady don't want to go out the way walking by the graveyard.

"Your grandma's buried out there. You been to see her?"

"No," I say. I don't tell her I don't go see nobody in the graveyard.

"Well, that makes two of us. Guess I'll make it there sooner or later. She's not going anywhere," she say and smile.

I don't smile and I don't say nuthin. What kind of woman don't come when her mama die, then come back home and smile?

"You think I'm hard, don't you? Hard to have left you. My mama. Pearl. Well, you think I'm bad, you should've met your grandmother."

She quiet after saying that, and we walk through town without talking.

"Hasn't nuthin here changed," she say after a while. "It's been twelve years. I bet all the folks at the church know I'm back and why."

I hold my hand to my mouth and act like I'm coughing. Miss Nola right. Most everybody did know she was coming back to town. And knew she didn't come when her mama died. But didn't nobody know why.

"That's the thing I love most about a city, Septeema. Don't nobody know who you are unless you tell them. You can walk down the street and never see nobody you know. Kind of like being invisible. Yeah, almost like not being real."

I think about that for a while. About being in some city where nobody know my name. About not having no MC, no Wilhelmina, no Douglass. Not having nobody to hold onto when I sleep. Not holding nobody else when they cry.

"Sound awful quiet up there," I say.

"It is quiet, here inside," she say, pointing to her head. "Some of the women at the lamp plant where I worked used to call me Silence."

"You didn't never talk?"

"Sometimes. Most times I just kept my mouth shut. Seems like life can do that to you sometimes, put so much on your mind till you can't even speak.

"A'Lelia Collins was the one got me out of my silence. She the one give me my fur coat and a lot of fancy dresses. She gave them to me when her daughter died and looking good didn't matter to her no more.

"A'Lelia'd been working in a factory ever since they first let colored women get other work besides farming or day work. She used to be a trackwoman on the Baltimore and Ohio railroad before she came to Chicago.

"I got a picture of her holding a shovel almost as big as she is.

"She a friend to me. More of a mama than my own was. Gets on me all the time about doing right by you, since her daughter died before she could do right by her.

"A'Lelia helped me find the words inside myself. The words I can know myself by and feel strong in the world. Now what's your story?"

"Miss Marius say she sent you letters about me," I say.

"I burned them," she say.

"Well, what you wanna know about me now for, then?" I ask.

She act like she don't know what to say. I don't neither, but I gotta let her know I know she didn't wanna know nuthin about me. Not then or now. She got something up her sleeve, I can feel it.

"I wasn't burning you. It was my past I tried to burn from my mind. But you know what?"

I don't look at her, don't say nuthin.

"I found out things don't work like that. The past can sneak up on you even when you think you've left it behind. It can be standing around a corner waiting for you to come, then it'll jump out and scare you to death. Funny thing is, I didn't think there was any scared left in me."

We walk a ways further without talking. Now that I know some called her Silence, I feel good not talking. I shift what she say about the past around inside my head. Even bad as I think about Lucille some time, I still wouldn't burn her out of my mind. And she ain't even blood.

"You love Pearl, don't you, Septeema?"

"I guess so."

"Funny, I never even thought about you loving this place. When I was your age all I could dream about was leaving. Me and your daddy almost made it out together."

"My daddy didn't wanna be here with you or me. He left, killed hisself in the woods, that's what Lucille say. My daddy didn't leave nuthin in the world but me."

"And me," she say softly.

"How come all my life gotta be wrapped up around you all of a sudden?"

"Septeema, I hope one day soon you'll understand."

I make my mouth into a long hard line. I ain't never gonna understand nuthin she got to say. Never gonna understand it. Never.

"My name is Raisin, don't nobody call me Septeema," I say.

"Your name is Septeema and that's what I'm going to call you," she say.

We stop walking. I look at her, she look at me. Something small move in her eyes, water standing in em make em extra shiny. Everything about this woman shine: her legs, her long arms without the fur coat, them pearly dark glasses, the promise in her mouth not spoken, never spoken.

"Don't nobody love you, you know." There, I said it. Got out that hot thing pressing inside my chest.

"I didn't always love my mama neither. That's part of the reason I'm here."

I take off down the road then, running.

"I'm still your mama, no matter how fast you run, no matter how far you go. I'm still YOUR M-A-M-A!" she call out after me.

I let her words fall behind me like water off a duck's back. I pick my legs up and turn em fast as they can turn on the road. I don't care if she get lost, don't care if she slip and break her neck on them high-heel shoes. What kind of woman is this woman, and what kind of child am I?

III

▼

I RUN TILL I'M ON THE STRETCH OF ROAD between Miss Dubois's and Miss Lomax's. I bend over till my chest almost touch my knees and try to catch my breath.

Then it come back, that heavy feeling come back on me. And the voices, louder now—stronger cause I let em in when I start listening to Nola Barnett. My legs won't move and my head fill up with sound. I see Miss Nola walking slow on the road, then I don't see nuthin but liquid black. Something move in me, warm, but not blood. That man voice say, "Never gonna leave you now, Baby Girl. Not you, not your mama. Not again."

My hands turn into cups and my arms raise up in the air. I feel Miss Nola walking on the road, Miss Nola moving closer to me, steady in them sharp black shoes. She lean toward me and shake me a bit. She look in my eyes and I wonder what she see. Me? Or my daddy? Who she really love—me or him in me?

I smell the mint in her mouth. And something else. Some old bitter smell fall over my face like a veil. I try to open my mouth. Want to scream but my lips closed tight.

"Septeema, Raisin? You hear me?" Miss Nola ask.

I can't even nod my head, just look at her, feel her with my eyes closed.

Water rushing in my head now and something old. Something whispering behind my eyes, "PUHPUH, PUHPUH, PUHPUH, PUH-PUH . . . ," old sharp whispery sound and I can't scream. Somebody inside me. Somebody here inside my head. My lips turn around her name. I open my lips to say her name but they don't move, they closed and somebody here inside me. I can't get out her name.

"PUHPUH, PUHPUH, PUHPUH, PUHPUH . . . " I try to make my body fall, my arms, my legs, don't nuthin move.

Miss Nola grab hold of one my arms and rub it, soft soft but that old water's still moving and I can't see who's in it swimming inside my eyes and the black change to red now and Miss Nola grab my other arm and rub it too. I feel her soft dry skin in all this heat and she standing here in the middle of the road rubbing my arms, she don't even know me, this woman say she my mama and I can't even move my lips. My head feel heavy from all this water and "PUHPUH, PUHPUH, PUHPUH, PUHPUH . . . " sharp as Miss Nola Barnett's heels in my ears. I holler and she pull me to her then, tight. She say, "Septeema, Septeema, I'm your mama and you're going to be all right. All right. I'm not going to let you be taken from me like El took himself!"

And my eyes open and see the water standing in hers and she looking inside me through all that water and stroking my back like I'm a soft furry thing inside one of her satchels. And inside my mind I say, Mama? You my mama? But I can't let it slip out into the air where she might hear and catch and turn the words into something pointy that stings.

I V

▼

S HE STROKE ME TILL I STOP SHAKING and ain't nobody but me inside my head.

"This ever happen to you before?"

I shake my head no. Don't want her to know bout earlier today on the way to meet her, don't want her to know I'm scairt.

"We're going to have to talk about this, you know. It doesn't have to be now, but it's going to have to be soon."

"No."

"I think I can help you, baby. Help you understand."

"Ain't nuthin for me to understand. Nuthin at all. I got dizzy from running, that's all. Sick and dizzy from running."

"More than running got into you, Septeema. I saw it. I felt it. And I think I understand it."

I look at this woman like she crazier than me. How she gonna understand anything about me when she ain't seen me most of my life? I don't even think she understand herself. I start wondering, how am I gonna get away from Miss Nola Barnett?

"Is there someplace around here where we can sit awhile and talk?"

"I wanna get home to Miss Marius."

"I've got to rest for a minute. Come on."

I let her hold my hand and lead me into the cool of the trees. She find a spot with light coming through and a open nurse log. She sit, but I stand up.

"There's something you need to know. Something I need to tell you about your daddy and me," she start.

"You coulda wrote it in a letter," I say.

"No. This is something I have to tell you face-to-face."

"So?" I ask, watching that something catch in her throat.

"It's not an easy thing to tell. Not something I can just open my mouth and say."

"Well, if you can't say it, how I'm gonna know it?" I ask.

"I can say it. I just need to ease into the telling, that's all."

"Miss Marius gonna be worried."

"Miss Marius knows you're with your mama," she say.

"But she don't know what either one of us might do," I say.

"I bet she knows both of us better than you think."

"She know me like a mama."

"But she knows I am your mama," she say.

"So you say."

"You always talk like this to grown folk?" she ask.

"Only grown folk that talk to me like you."

"I see you got the Barnett mouth. Good. You're going to need it in this life."

I see she gonna keep going around till she ready to say whatever she got to, so I sit down on the ground.

"The lake's not far from here, is it?"

I shake my head no.

"You swim?"

"No."

"You shouldn't live around so much water and not be able to swim."

Now she gonna start telling me what to do.

"One thing I did forget was how it smelled out here, the water, the trees, the green. Make you think anything can happen. Think you can be anything, smelling all this green. And that's exactly what happened to El and me."

"El?"

"Your daddy."

"Oh." What else could I say? Didn't nobody never try to tell me nuthin much about the man till now. Grown folks don't like young ones asking em a bunch of questions. Just grunt and say, "You'll understand it all one day." Miss Marius say it ain't her place to talk about my daddy's business. She was leaving that story for my mama to tell.

"We were going to get married. Lord, I used to spend so much time worrying over how I was going to look in a wedding dress. I wasn't nowhere near as pretty as my mama, even though El said I was. She kept a picture of my daddy and her in a gold frame on her bureau. They looked like something out of a picture show. Black suit, white shirt, big black bow tie. A high-necked white lace dress and sparkly earrings. And their smiles even brighter than the jewels in her ears. I wanted to look like that. Happy. Proud. Pretty. But I just couldn't see myself in her."

I move around a bit on the ground, pick at the dirt with a stick.

"My daddy had a problem, a secret he kept to himself. One day I found out what it was, but by then my mother knew about it too."

I look up into the tops of the trees, look up into the sky.

"It's important that you know these things, Septeema. So mistakes we made, you won't have to carry in your life."

"I ain't gonna carry nobody's mistakes but mine," I say.

"That's what I thought too, Septeema. But I was wrong. And I stopped believing in any kind of god a long time ago, but in church they always said the sins of the fathers would be visited upon the children, and I found out that saying was true."

"You don't believe in God?" I know Miss Marius ain't gonna like me sitting in the woods with nobody who don't believe in God. "Miss Marius know that?"

"I'm grown, Septeema. I have a right to what I believe same as anybody else, including Miss Marius. And I also have the right for my beliefs to be respected, same as I respect anybody else's."

"But how can you not believe in God?" I know this woman crazy now. Those words more scary to me than them whispers in my body.

"The suffering going on in the world makes me believe God's nuthin but a coward. Why else is all this pain free to run loose in the world?"

I don't want God to think I think like this crazy woman.

"But that ain't God, that's man causing the suffering. That's what Miss Marius always say. Folks all the time doing wrong then turning around and putting it on God."

"They cowards just like God," she say.

I don't want to talk about God like this, so I ask, "What kind of secret your daddy have?"

Nola Barnett shift her large body on the log. She stretch her arms and hold the round red tips of her fingers into the air and inspect them slowly, one by one. She act like she don't want to answer.

"You got a boyfriend?"

Why she all the time wanna get into my business? She know I ain't got no boyfriend.

"No," all I say.

"You want one?"

"No." Now she really starting to make me mad.

"Well, you might change your mind after while. But one thing I want you to remember is can't nobody fill you up."

"Huh?"

"My daddy had a hole in him so big that lake couldn't fill it up. You know what a gourd is?"

"No," I say.

"It's a shell on certain kind of fruit. It's carved out and hollow on the inside. Some places they put beads and things on the outside and you can shake them and make music. Other places they use them to dip water. People can be like that, something beaded and musical. And empty inside. My mother didn't hear the rattle inside my daddy, the dry shake and roll of his bones.

"When she heard the first clatter, I was seven years old. My daddy came to me once, late at night, before I was dreaming. He brushed my cheek with his lips, told me to look inside his eyes. 'You can't see it, can you?' he whispered. 'Nobody sees it, cause nuthin is there.' And then he laughed as loud as I've ever heard anybody laugh.

" 'I'll tell you a secret,' he said. 'A secret nobody knows. This is not my real face. My eyes, the lips, the nose, none of it's real. Go on, touch it, pull it. I bet it comes loose in your hands. Don't be afraid, there ain't nuthin behind it, if you pull it off.'

"I touched the water on his face. He put my fingers to his lips, kissed them. Two months later he was dead."

"How did he die?" I ask.

"My aunt told me your grandma shot him."

"Oh," all I say.

"In a way, he was right, Septeema. His face wasn't real, none of our faces are real. My face doesn't tell you who I really am, or why I'm here."

I feel even more scairt of this woman. Her face look too real and too close. Won't nobody hear me in these woods if I scream.

"You don't understand now why I'm telling you this. But one day you will. One day you'll have questions about the whos and the whys and I want to be the one tell you the answers."

"Well, we gonna have plenty of answering to do to Miss Marius if we don't get home soon," I say.

"All right, Septeema. I'll try to wait till you're ready, but I can't promise I will. I don't like what I saw on the road back there."

And I don't like what I see sitting on this log right here.

V

▼

WE GET UP AND MOVE through the trees to the road. I don't want to talk, just make my legs move fast as they can whether she keep up or not.

"Will you walk down to the lake with me tomorrow?" I hear her call from somewhere behind me. I act like I don't hear.

"Septeema, will you take me to the lake tomorrow? There's something I've got to see."

All the time, it's what she want. She want to leave Pearl, she go. She want to come to Pearl, she come. She want to burn the letters, she do. She want to call me Septeema. She want to be my mama now. She want to give me answers, she want to ask questions. She want to walk home, she want to see the lake. Well, I don't want none of it. None of her smiles, her gifts, her stories. Don't want to walk nowhere and don't want to talk about nuthin. I throw the mirror in the dirt and walk faster.

Only a black snake moving cross the road slow me down.

I look at the snake and wish. To be long and black and something that hiss. Something that coil. To be something that creep up on things quietly. Wrap around a body and squeeze. To take Nola Barnett into my mouth and swallow her body, then fall asleep for weeks.

"You dropped this," Miss Nola Barnett say, holding the mirror in her hand.

I turn. A hiss form in my mouth. My spit burn like poison. Skin on my back start to stretch. I feel long.

"I'll hold it for you till we get to Miss Marius's. I know we don't have too much farther to go," she say after looking at my face.

She hold the mirror tight like I do. I turn around and keep walking. She walk fast now with me. Still walking steady in them shoes.

"When I was young I wanted to be just like my mother," she say, huffing a bit. "Wanted to be pretty like her. I didn't know then what I know now about beauty, about it being what you feel about yourself on the inside. That's where the real beauty is. In knowing and believing in yourself. Back then I didn't care nuthin about that stuff. I wanted to be pretty like everybody said my mama was. Like I thought she was. On the outside."

This woman ain't never gonna stop telling me about things I don't want to know.

"One time when I was talking to her about wishing I was pretty, she told me a story about a healing stone. You ever hear it?"

"No," I say. But she don't see the please don't in my face. She start telling the story while we walk.

"Well, a long time ago an old woman and her daughter lived in a little raggedy house by the lake. The daughter wouldn't ever leave the house because she had all kinds of marks and scars on her face and she didn't want anybody besides the old woman to see her. The old woman was getting worried about her daughter not leaving the house, because she knew she was going to die soon and was looking forward to dying and didn't want to worry about her daughter after she was gone. The mother was the one who got their food and anything else they needed.

"'What will you do when I'm gone, daughter?' she'd ask.

"'You're not going anywhere,' the daughter always answered.

"The morning of the day she knew she was to die, the old woman called her daughter to her bed.

"'I'll be gone by nightfall, daughter. Are you ready to do what you must do?'

"The daughter looked at her mother laying in the bed. Her mother's strong face was gone now. Instead the daughter saw a face she didn't want to understand. The old woman touched her daughter's face lightly.

"'Nothing's as beautiful to me as your face, daughter. But you haven't believed me. You think a smooth cold skin would warm my heart, could give the joy your smile brings me? No. But you are the one who must choose. To live your life alone in this house, or move out into the world. Now I'll find peace as I must find it, you will come to your own. Outside the door a whole world awaits you. To open the door demands faith.'

"The daughter sat beside her mother's bed, holding her hand and singing the old songs her mother loved. She was still singing when her mother's spirit left the house. The daughter cried for weeks after her mother's death, but she still wouldn't open the door and leave the house, not even to bury the old woman's body.

"Finally, after the stink from the old woman's dead body was so strong the daughter felt death was moving from her mother's bed into her own, she slowly opened the door and jumped. The old woman had left a note for her hanging on a string in the doorway.

> Daughter, I'm glad you've chosen life. Don't go back inside the house. Don't eat for five days. The morning of the sixth day wash yourself in fresh water. Fasten a rope to a large stone and tie the rope to your waist. Get into our boat and row to the middle of the lake. Sing an old song loud as you can. Drop the stone in the water. You'll sink to Changer's house inside the hole at the bottom of the lake. Tell her what you came for, what you want most in the world.

"The daughter did as she was told. After singing the old song, she dropped the stone into the water and went down to Changer's house, deep inside the hole in the bottom of the lake. Changer had the shape and size of a woman, a small woman with hair that moved like waves. She asked the daughter if she was pure, if she had her heart in the right place. The daughter said yes.

"Changer asked her what she wanted most in the world and the daughter told her, beauty. Changer took the stone at the end of the rope that was tied to the daughter's waist and rubbed the stone gently against the daughter's skin. Then Changer unfastened the rope and the daughter floated out of the hole in the bottom of the lake and up to the water's surface. The daughter put her fingers to her face to touch the bumps and scars, but they were gone.

"She swam to shore and began the long walk into town. She never went back to the house she had shared with her mother by the lake. She never went inside those sad four walls again."

"She sound crazy to me," I say as we turn into Miss Marius's yard.

"I used to think she was crazy myself. But when my mother

told me that story all I wanted to do was get inside a boat and go out on the lake to the middle and sing. I thought that if I jumped in the water and went to the bottom of the lake I could find that stone and rub it on my face and I'd be pretty.

"But my mother knew I was scared of the water and she didn't worry about me trying nuthin like that. She thought I'd learn to be satisfied about the way I looked if I saw it couldn't be changed easy."

Miss Nola Barnett finally quiet. I think about what she say about her wanting to be pretty. I look at her smooth black skin and glossy eyes, her soft lashes and shiny red lips. She lying. She gots to be. Just like she lying about being my mama and wanting to know about me. She got something standing behind her eyes, some kind of shadow I just can't see.

"I started thinking something bad happened . . . " Miss Marius say opening the door and grabbing Miss Nola's arm to pull her in the house. Miss Nola turn and look and smile. She the only one hear the whisper,

"Me too. . . ."

SECTION 5

Blood Memory

I

Nola

▼

NOLA TWISTED IN THE OLD WHITE SHEETS on Miss Marius's bed.
She hadn't dreamed of her mother in years. Her mother had
been so real Nola could smell the lilac scent of her body, even
now. She sat up and eased her tired legs over the side of the high
wooden bed. She never should have suggested walking from the
train depot, she thought, as her toes pulsed in a wrathful chorus.

The girl would not be easy.

She had figured on some small anger, not this cool indifference, this sugar-coated fury inside a shell.

She would have to break her open, find some small hole and
push through. She did not have much time. She could feel him,
see the shape of him in the heavy Pearl air. There on the road she
could've almost touched him. She knew El was near.

She moved to the front window and pressed her face against a
cool pane. The sky began to break into fiery colors. She tried to

recall the song her father used to sing to her so many years ago, some sad song about red moons and people turning in on themselves. Though she focused on that memory and the picture of him she carried inside her mind, she could not invoke the sound of his voice.

She walked softly out of Miss Marius's room and down the hall to the room Septeema shared with the other children. She opened the door and stepped inside.

The light breathing of the children surprised her. They slept like those a breath away from stepping into other worlds.

Septeema took up the least space in the big bed. She slept on her side, back to the others, arms hugging her body as if she were protecting herself, even in sleep.

Nola touched her face lightly. Septeema did not stir.

"She's El all over," she whispered, surprised. "El and her grandma, for sure."

Nola lowered her face to Septeema's. She smelled the warm metallic scent of hate in Septeema's mouth.

Septeema opened one eye, then the other, and stared. Nola brushed her lips against her cheek and straightened, then walked quickly from the room.

I I

▼

THE DAYS FOLLOWING NOLA'S RETURN settled into an uneasy rhythm. Septeema did not come around Nola unless she was asked. Nola caught Septeema looking at her sometimes, but she never tried to talk to Nola, or smile.

"The girl don't talk?" Nola finally asked Miss Marius one day when her patience had almost run out.

"Give her time, Nola. You something new, that's all."

"How much time is she going to need?"

"Well, you've been gone what, twelve, almost thirteen years? That's all her life, you know."

"Don't seem like but a minute."

"But it's been all of her life."

"All of hers, about half of mine. Damn, I didn't think it would take so long."

"Neither did we, Nola. Neither did we. Try to see what it must be like for her."

* * *

Nola watched the girl they called Raisin, the girl she called by her given name, Septeema. The girl that came out of her body. Hers. Not the one she was always running to, the one she leaned up against and hugged. No matter how good Miss Marius was, the girl belonged to her.

See what it must be like, Miss Marius had said.

Must be for her what it is for me, Nola thought while walking quickly, angrily through the trees.

El was out here. She could feel him calling her, pulling her on.

"What you want with me now, El? I come for the girl like you asked, ain't that enough?" Nola called out to the trees. "All I wanted was to be left alone, you hear me? ALONE! Didn't want no baby fooling round me, didn't want nobody knowing my name. And here you come, up behind me all the time, wanting. What about me, huh? What about what I want?"

Nola stumbled into a clearing in the trees. She stood in a circle of light in the green. She raised a hand into the air, pointed toward the apex of the sun, then turned in a slow hot circuit.

"You think I'm going to do what you say? Follow behind you, like a child? Well, I' grown. A woman now, boy. You watch and see what I'm gonna do."

Nola turned around and stomped her way back to Miss Marius's. Septeema was sitting on the front porch with the girl with the mark on her face. They both looked down when Nola walked into the yard. The big girl, Lucille, turned a corner on the house, running. She stopped dead still when she saw Nola.

"Something wrong, Miss Nola? Raisin done made some offense?" Lucille asked.

Nola didn't respond, just walked up to the porch.

"We're going to the lake, Septeema."

Raisin looked at Nola, but made no effort to move.

"I don't feel like going right now," Raisin said.

"We're going to the lake now, Septeema. I've waited long enough."

"You want me to get Miss Marius, Miss Nola? She'll get the sour out of Raisin," Lucille said.

"No. Thank you, Lucille. I don't need Miss Marius to take care of this."

"You ought to be glad you got a mama come for you, pretty as she is. Ain't nobody else sides Miss Marius gonna put up with you," Lucille said.

Raisin looked at Lucille the same way she'd been looking at Nola. The girl with the mark touched her on the arm.

"You better go, Raisin," was all Wilhelmina said.

Nola watched Septeema sit back against the house, pulling herself inside herself. Raisin closed her eyes and for a long minute nobody said a word. When Lucille was ready to burst from wanting to run and get Miss Marius, Septeema stood up and walked out of the yard, headed for the trees.

"You better slow down, girl. Miss Nola can't walk fast as you," Lucille called out to Raisin's rigid back.

But Lucille was wrong. Nola could walk as fast as Septeema, she was mad enough to walk a quick hundred miles. The two angry kinswomen walked into the soothing dark of the trees. Their haughty footsteps on the dry red road were the only noises heard beneath peaceful woodsounds.

Nola watched the girl's stiff back.

She'll break before she bends, Nola thought. Well, if that's the way it has to be . . .

I I I

▼

AFTER THEY HAD WALKED SO FAR into the trees Nola couldn't tell where they were, she detected the faint scent of fresh water.

"I can smell it," she called out to Septeema's back.

Septeema walked without responding, and soon they stepped from the dark of the trees onto the rocky-edged ring around the lake, whose luminous black was as inviting as a dream.

A multitude of memories hit Nola's body like a wall of waves. El on and in the water, silver streaks of fish in buckets, the steam from a low red sun, soothing black water on her troubled brown body, healing laughter, the holiness of silence.

She was not immune. The long fingers of sorrow gently stroked her brow. She would not let the girl see her tears. She would not let that old dead thing crawl back into her body, into her opening soul. She was about to do what she had come to do, about to free herself, the girl. She would not let that thing in. She would not cry. She would not break. She would not bow down to that grasping emptiness. She would not.

A sun burned and swelled inside her head. She dropped to the softly pebbled earth and held her head in her hands. An old song her mother used to sing burst from her lips:

Oh-oh, run run mourner run
bright angels above . . .

She didn't care what the girl thought now. She didn't care if there were a hundred gods or one, if history reached no further than her fingertips, if time was unresponsive as the eternally silent lake. She didn't care if her mama had never told her everything was going to be all right, never told her she loved her, never even saw Nola outside of her daddy's name. She didn't care if she went back to Chicago, into the black water or straight to hell.

I would fly away to the kingdom
bright angels above
if I just had two wings
bright angels above . . .

She felt that old ugly thing grab hold and dig its fingers into her soul. Twelve years of silence, so old it lay in her body like a subterranean lake of fire. She thought she had covered it over, filled the hole with the mud of her life since Pearl.

Now she felt it rising: the burning silence, the liquid pain, the agony rising from the fissure inside, rising, gathering heat and steam, and a wild uncontrollable energy.

You gotta escape for your life
bright angels above
you just gotta escape for your life
bright angels above
oh-oh, run run mourner run
bright angels above . . .

Nola did not feel Septeema sit next to her and take hold of
one hand, then the other. She did not see the tears she could not
shed for herself wetting her daughter's face.

Once she ended the old song, her mother's favorite, she
wailed until the sound of a cry took shape and rolled over the
lake's still waters, then flew into the air as if the sound had wings
as it flew above the eavesdropping trees.

Still no tears would come. Her wail had loosened something
inside her, though, something that allowed her to look into her
daughter's face and truly see her for the first time.

"Did I come all this way for you to tell me I really don't have
nobody? Not nobody in this world?" Nola asked.

Septeema took her hands from Nola's and dried her face.
She didn't answer.

"You wait. Wait till you see what it feels like. Miss Marius
and Nathan aren't blood. There's things, girl, running deep
inside you. Deep inside. That's what blood is, something run
deep. You don't even know about the people's blood in you.

"Their stories are there . . . all there. The love, the hate,
good times and bad. My people. Your daddy's people. They're all
in there. Inside your blood.

"Listen sometime, they're trying to talk to you. Why do you
think I'm here?"

"That's one thing I been wondering ever since Miss Marius
showed me the letter said you was coming," Raisin said, pulling
her body back a ways from Nola.

"I came because of your daddy."

"But you said my daddy was dead."

"Your daddy is dead."

Nola struggled with what she wanted, needed, to tell Raisin. The white look on Raisin's face showed her how hard the telling was going to be.

"Your daddy would've been a fine man. A fine one. He was kind, and had a gentleness I've never seen in a man since. He wasn't nuthin like the men who can be so full of themselves that they don't have room for anybody else inside."

"How did he die?" Raisin asked.

"He couldn't see a way to hold on to the light inside himself and live in this world," Nola said, scratching her head.

Raisin's troubled look made Nola explain.

"He would've had to go into the mine. Old Number 9. Would've had to take his light down in that hole in the ground like all the other colored men.

"Cept he said he couldn't do it. Not for me. Not for you. Say all that was waiting for a colored man in this world was a hole somewhere, some hellhole in the ground.

"Said if he had to be buried alive, he'd do it himself. Laid his body down like them old Africans he was always talking about. Laid his body down just like them. Found a spot, dug a hole, and laid his tired body down. He remembered the words and the ways—the plants that should only be used for healing, but could also call down death. He never should've done it, killing yourself is against the old ways. But he was set on dying. He wanted his soul to rise and walk away from his bones.

"Ain't nuthin but a line," he was always saying. "Nuthin but a line holding this world back from the next."

"Is all my people crazy?" Raisin asked in a whisper.

"Sometimes I think El got good sense. The times when I feel there's nuthin for me in this world. Most times, though, I know he was wrong. He had something waiting in this world. He had me and you. We're plenty to live for, right?"

Raisin didn't answer.

"I didn't know what he was talking about either. Thought all this love could hold him back." Nola snorted like a tired horse.

"I tried to tell him, though. Tried to tell him like the Reverend always say, he wasn't never gonna find peace if he crossed that line. But he didn't listen to me. Some part of me hoped he was just talking to hear himself talk. Once he decided to raise his boots and cross that line, wasn't nobody able to hold him back.

"After he died, I cried until my body ached. Then I got mad. Wild, crazy mad. The only thing that would soothe my anger was silence.

"Till A'Lelia. And I still get mad at him. You'll probably feel mad sometimes, too."

Nola stopped talking and was silent. Raisin sat with her eyes closed. Nola looked hard at Septeema's bowed head. She couldn't wait any longer, even if the girl might not be ready.

Nola saw the hard-edged anger in Raisin's body. She could feel the rejection rising off Raisin's skin. First her daddy had left her, then Nola, too.

"Before he died, he told me it would be important for me to remember some things, to call his name and say prayers for him after he was gone. I didn't pay him no mind."

Septeema raised her head, her face full of questions—if she was good enough, pretty enough, would they have stayed with her? It would be a while before Raisin could believe anything Nola had to say.

"But I knew his spirit wasn't ever going to rest after he killed himself."

Septeema put her head back down.

"He wanted special words said from the Old Ones he was

always talking about. He wanted the charms he wore around his neck laid on his grave. Wanted some old songs sung, rattles shaken, a drum beaten, and dancing around the grave. You ever see a funeral like that in Pearl?"

"No. I don't even go to the graveyard. Not for nuthin, or nobody," Raisin said.

"Your daddy wanted me to do these things. It would be nice if you'd do them now, with me."

"Since he dead, he ain't gonna know I don't do it."

"He'd like it if you were there."

"But he dead, this don't make no sense."

"Septeema, I don't want to scare you, but your daddy means for you to take part. Who you think got into you back on the road?"

"But how can a dead man know me, or care what I do?"

"I didn't used to believe the dead bothered with us myself. But I know there's things in the world, Septeema, can't none of us explain. I know me coming here and telling you this is making you upset, but we don't have much time."

"What you mean?"

"That's all I want to say now. I want you to think about what I've told you, then let me know your decision."

"Decision about what? Ain't nuthin to decide."

"Just think about what I've said."

"All right," Raisin said, standing. "We better get back home, we got a long way to go."

Nola looked at the girl who had comforted her a short while ago. The girl who had stroked Nola in a moment of acute distress.

You wouldn't have known we'd even touched, Nola thought as she watched the stiffness return to Septeema's body, as she headed back through the trees. Septeema had an unseen bundle atop her head that she unknowingly carried back to Miss Marius.

I V

▼

"WHAT KIND OF FOOLISHNESS you putting in that girl's head?" Nola slowly opened her eyes. Miss Marius towered over her in the bed, her face a mask of fury.

"What?"

"I say what kind of foolishness you putting in that girl's head?"

"What I tell my child is between me and her. This don't have nuthin to do with you."

"I done raised that child almost thirteen years. Thirteen years, you hear me? Everything about her's got something to do with me."

"I don't care if you raised her a hundred years, she's still mine, Miss Marius, mine! You might've raised her, but I birthed her."

"Who wanted her born?"

"I was fifteen. Didn't know nuthin about nuthin. Lost the one person in the world who loved me."

"You always had somebody else who loved you."

"Who, Miss Marius? You were there, tell me. Who?"

"You know your mama loved you. You still twisted up inside your head and you too blind to see it."

"My mama had me to keep hold of my daddy. When that didn't work, she didn't want nuthin to do with me."

"You don't know what you're talking about. Done run off somewhere and got your mind messed up worse than it was when you left. Your mama loved you and your daddy. Her love just got turned around inside her head, is all. Love can make you feel crazy, do crazy."

"She was crazy behind my daddy, Miss Marius. Don't you know that by now?"

"Just like you crazy behind some boy dead twelve years."

Miss Marius opened the door and listened for the sleeping sounds of the house. Satisfied, she closed the door.

Nola got out of the bed and slipped on her robe, belting it with short, angry jerks. Miss Marius pulled a chair next to the bed and sat.

"You might as well sit too," Miss Marius said. "We got all night to get this settled."

"How are we going to settle this tonight?" Nola asked. "We're talking about almost thirteen years."

"We're talking about that child's life," Miss Marius said.

"My child."

"You got a nerve, Nola. Nathan told me to leave it alone. Said let it be and what's right would come to pass. But I raised that child and loved her like I would've loved my own if I'd been blessed enough to have my own.

"And we waited for you. Both of us. We waited, Nola. One

year, she walking and talking, five years, she going to school, still waiting. Cause I told her from early on that I was just Miss Marius and she got a mama coming for her. But you didn't never come, Nola. Not never. You just sent me a address from time to time. Nuthin for her. Not one visit, one call on the telephone, one line on a scrap of paper. Not once in almost thirteen years. Till now.

"Now you got something you want from her, so you come. Not to see how she's doing, not to see how not having the mama she was told is real and coming for her, not come, and how that made her feel. Not seeing the hole of that mama's absence that broke her up so bad inside, the girl don't even halfway talk right.

"Did you ever once think about that there in Chicago while you worrying behind that dead boy and what your dead mama did to you? Did you ever once stop and think about the live kin you got, that come outta your body, the girl you tried to burn up inside yourself? Did you ever once stop, and think maybe your hands ain't clean?"

"Why you think I'm here?"

"You can't wipe the slate like that, Nola. Nice as it would be if you could. I've been here for every one of these twelve years. And every one was a hard year for her, every year took something, Nola. Something precious she was gonna need to be whole."

"And I'm here to start giving back."

"You're here to keep taking."

"I'm going to take her with me."

"No. You're not gonna take her nowhere."

"She's mine, Miss Marius. I didn't want it to have to be like this, but I'm going to take her. And can't nobody on this earth stop me."

Miss Marius was deadly still.

"Somebody can stop you."

"Who? You?" Nola laughed. "I ain't even worried about that."

"That's your biggest problem, Nola. Not worrying about things you need to be worried about."

Miss Marius rose from her chair and left the room without making a sound.

Nola went to the window and looked into the dark. She closed her eyes and saw her father walking on that same dirt road so many years ago. They were coming from the church picnic. Her father walked with his shoulders slumped, his head hanging down. Behind him was her mother, limping from the pinch of the shoes on her feet, a triumphant smile bright as a crown on her face. The smile she wore only for Nola's father. Nola saw herself walking slowly, slowly behind the two. Neither acknowledged her whimpering. Her father's pretty woman had given her the watermelon, the juicy red sprinkled with a powder that scorched her young tongue and burned her throat as it slid into her stomach, where it rested like a hot thing growing inside.

Nola saw the sun press the younger Nola into the dirt, the struggle of her youthful arms to catch herself, the pink river running from her mouth. Her tongue licking the road.

Her father had turned and run toward her, her mother had turned once, looked, and kept walking. Nola saw her father kneel and scoop, watched her young head roll, eyes going back. Then dark. Black as the night she looked out into now, dark as blood memory.

You coming? El asked from the dark, hungry.

"I told you I'd be there," Nola whispered into the glass.

V

▼

NOLA WOKE TO THE SOUND of scuffling in the front yard.
"Take it back!"

"Don't haveta!"

"Take it . . . "

"It's true!"

"You a lie!"

"Ask Miss Marius. Go on, ask her. You'll see it's true."

Nola urged her tired body out of bed and went to the window. Septeema and Lucille lay in the dirt below, huffing and puffing.

"I heard her tell Nathan. She didn't never want you and neither did Miss Nola. Didn't none of your mamas want you, why you think you're here?"

"Neither did yours. Least mine come back!"

"Not for you. She took one look at you and knew she couldn't take you nowhere. Miss Marius just felt sorry."

Septeema struggled under the weight of Lucille's great bulk. The two boys and the girl with the mark on her face stood in a broken circle around the two girls rolling in the dirt. When Septeema put her hands around Lucille's wide neck, hope washed over their faces.

Nola opened the window.

"You two there! Stop that fighting!"

The girls continued to twist and heave with increased urgency after hearing Nola's voice. Septeema tightened her grip on Lucille's neck while Lucille tried to free herself and force all of her weight on Septeema in an effort to crush her. By the time Nola reached them, Septeema was fast losing strength and Lucille's face had grown to mammoth proportions.

"Stop it right now. You two get up from there, wallowing on the ground like two hogs. Get up from there, right this minute. I know you both know better."

She helped both of them to their feet and brushed them off.

"I was only telling her the truth. The girl act like she got worse sense now that you're here," Lucille said, breathless.

"What's she saying got you mad enough to fight, Septeema?" Nola asked.

Lucille snickered and folded her arms across her heaving chest.

"She run her mouth too much, don't know what she talking about. Just talking to be talking. Don't none of us want to hear it," Septeema said.

"It's the truth."

"You a lie and ain't no truth in you," Septeema said, hot.

Lucille made a move as if to grab Septeema again, but Nola stepped between them.

"She think just because you're here, she can act uppity. She knows I'll wring her neck like a chicken if she keep talking crazy to me."

"Look like you the chicken," Septeema said.

MC, Wilhelmina, and Douglass whooped and ran out of the yard. Septeema followed them.

"Don't nobody around here love none of you, you know. Not nobody," Lucille called after the running, tittering four.

Septeema turned around and looked at Nola and Lucille, then she swung back and cackled, running for the trees.

"Why you like to say that?" Nola asked Lucille. "Miss Marius let you say any kind of hurting thing come into your mind to those children?"

Lucille hung her head, but didn't say a word.

"You're scared, aren't you? Scared Miss Marius don't have enough love left for you. Well, let me tell you something, child, love ain't like sand in a hourglass, it don't run out. If you're lucky, it grows and if you're not, well, then you've got something to worry about."

"I ain't telling no lies," Lucille said as she turned and walked quickly into the house.

Nola shook her head and was glad the thing would soon be done. She looked at what she thought would be the silhouette of four children walking down the road, but saw instead three children walking farther down the road, and a fourth, Septeema, standing stock still with her arms held out like her mother's faded picture of Jesus on the cross.

"I knew. I always knew he'd get her first," Nola said, running for the girl, who stood like a tree, forsaken on the road.

Ouida Barnett's voice, singing, began to ring inside Nola's ears.

Run run mourner run
bright angels above

oh-oh run run mourner run
bright angels above . . .

Beneath the singing, Ouida's voice asked the unspoken question in Nola's eyes.

What makes a woman forsake her child for a man?

If I had two wings
bright angels above
If I just had two wings
bright angels above . . .

Nola forced the sound of Ouida Barnett's singing from her mind. As she neared Septeema the air turned electric.

She tasted salt on her tongue. She ran with her eyes closed. Panting. She saw El's body turn. Falling. Turning around and over like the world. Then up. The body was up and moving. Out of endless black. The swirling black where dreams begin.

"Hold on, Septeema." Nola shouted through the static.

Behind El's body, Ouida Barnett laughed. A wild moaning laughter like a lowdown sun. Laughing. Mocking. Remembering.

"You better hold on," Nola's mother screamed, cackling.

The singing began again, louder.

Oh-oh, run run mourner run
bright angels above
oh-oh run run mourner run
bright angels above
I would fly away to the kingdom
if I just had two wings . . .

Nola could not push her mother away. She felt icy fingers on her soul. She was engulfed in a putrified cloud. The body stood. A body of dried skin over bones. Still as death. Still as Ouida Barnett's heart. Blood was on the rocks. A chant began: Paint the body red. Paint the body red. The body shook like a rattle. A holy gourd shaking. Its feet stomped the dry red earth. White teeth shining like polished bones. Her mother's mouth opened wide, singing:

> *You gotta escape for your life*
> *bright angels above*
> *you just gotta escape for your life*
> *bright angels above . . .*

The body stopped its stomping. Turned its hollow eyes on the girl. "ISSSSSS," it whistled. The air stopped moving. Nola couldn't breathe. She couldn't breathe and her mother was laughing. She fell into a numbness. The body beat the ground with a stick. Her mother beat the ground with a stick. "ISSSSSS," they whistled. Nola's father stood behind her mother behind the body. Light shining from the hole inside his chest. His face was a painted mask. Black. Red. He opened his mouth to join her mother singing,

> *Oh-oh, run run mourner run*
> *bright angels above*
> *Oh-oh, run run mourner run . . .*

The body held its bony fingers out to the girl. Her mother's song became part of Nola now. Bone. Flesh. Blood. Her feet hit the ground to its rhythm. She was the mourner on the road. Running. Running for her life, the girl's.

"Let her go. It's not her fault I left and didn't do what you wanted me to do. The blame belongs to me," Nola shouted at El's body, her mother and father, trying to get the girl.

"I came back, didn't I? Can't you see I came back? I'm gonna settle my accounts. I left all of you, but didn't I come back? I came back to claim my child before this blood memory steals her from me, from even herself. I came back to keep my baby girl with the living, not the dead."

They all stepped back. Into the darkness. Into the watery black.

Running till she could almost fly, Nola reached Septeema, grabbed her, stroked her wrinkled skin as if by touch she would learn who Septeema truly was. As the other children looked on, astonished, Nola held Septeema in her arms and told her over and over, till the sound of Nola's voice turned gentle as a waterwheel as she stroked the girl's arms down, wiped the terror from her face and rocked her gently, saying the words till they sounded like a song, "It's all right. It's all right. We're gonna be all right."

▼▼▼▼▼▼▼▼▼▼▼▼▼▼▼▼▼▼▼▼▼▼▼▼

SECTION 6

The Color of Spirits

▲▲▲▲▲▲▲▲▲▲▲▲▲▲▲▲▲▲▲▲▲▲▲▲

I

Sin-Sin

▼

WHAT TOOK YOU so long, boy?"
Sin-Sin looked at Blue sitting on a broken piece of wood.
He looked at the knife gleaming in his hand. The wood was the
color of Blue's dark skin.

"How you like it?"

"I like it fine."

"What you looking funny for then?"

"I didn't think you thought I was ready."

"Well. Now what you think?"

"Can you be ready and not know it?"

"Ain't but one way to know that, boy."

Sin-Sin hoped Blue didn't see the trembling that had started
in his left leg. Hard as he tried, he couldn't make his leg stay still.
He remembered all Blue had told him about not showing pain or
fear, how he had to keep his sorrow inside.

"What you say to my mother?" Sin-Sin asked.

"I told her she'd done a good job making a boy out of you, and asked her if I could help a bit with making you into a man."

"She didn't get mad?"

"She a smart woman. She ain't gonna get mad about the truth."

"She said what you're doing is like what a daddy would do," Sin-Sin said.

"Nope. She wrong about that. A daddy can't do what I'm gonna do for you. Most daddys'd try to make you into something like them. I'm gonna help you be you."

"I know something about my daddy."

"Boy, you don't know nuthin about your daddy," Blue snorted. "If you did, you wouldn't walk around here all the time looking sorry for yourself. First time I see you, I ask myself, who is that boy walking around here like he got a hole in his soul? Dragging your feet, head hanging down low. Couldn't be nuthin else that made you look like that."

Sin-Sin turned his back on Blue.

"We going down by the water like you said?" he asked.

Blue didn't say another word, he stood and started walking, the bones on his necklace rattling.

Sin-Sin followed Blue slowly. His left leg still felt wobbly and now his right arm was feeling shaky. He wondered if he'd be able to go through with it, be able to take the knife on his skin without screaming.

Mama's little baby . . .

The memory of the sound of the girls' voices began to fill his head. He stopped walking and shook his head, violently. He had to get rid of it, it couldn't follow him here, now, in the woods.

shortnin, shortnin . . .

Sin-Sin turned away from Blue as the taunting song swelled inside his head. He started running. Away from the woods, from the one who would give him what he wanted most in the world— to be a man and have a place in the world.

He heard the sound of Blue's voice carried by the wind through the trees. "What's wrong with you, boy?" He didn't stop, or turn around to answer.

I I

▼

FOR A TIME, Sin-Sin stayed away from the woods cause he might see Blue. He could see his mother wanted to question him about Blue, but he held his body in a stiff pose around her, so she wouldn't ask him any questions. And he was glad she didn't.

One chilly afternoon, he decided to sit in the woods and try to listen like Blue had told him.

"You have to learn how to listen to the woods, boy. Slowly. Carefully. With all the respect you got."

"But I don't hear nuthin."

"That's cause you ain't listening. You got to be able to listen to hear. What you hear now?"

"Birds. A branch or something, falling. Leaves."

"Anybody can hear that. I want you to listen to what's underneath those sounds."

"Ain't nuthin under them sounds."

"You keep listening. Pretty soon something's gonna start talking."

Sin-Sin had laughed a little and shook his head. No matter how long he sat in the woods, he heard the same sounds he always heard.

Finally, he had to change positions because of the cramps in his legs, and as soon as he shifted his body, he heard something. Footsteps headed towards him.

He tried to jump up so he could run, but got tangled up in his legs, folded beneath him. Too late, a young wrinkled face peered angrily at him from behind a tree.

"Can't go nowhere around here without some old dumb body getting in the way."

Sin-Sin stared at Raisin, relieved she wasn't Blue.

"What you mad about? I ain't done nuthin to you," he said.

"You ain't done nuthin for me either, but that don't make no difference. How come you always in my secret place?" She asked.

"I don't see no name on these trees," Sin-Sin said.

"Thought you liked to stay up under that wanga-man. What you doing out in these parts of the woods?"

Sin-Sin started to say something, then changed his mind.

"You turned into a man yet?"

"Nope."

"Then what you doing hanging around here?"

"Tending my business and leaving yours alone," Sin-Sin said.

"Well, good, then. You won't be bothering me and I won't be bothering you," Raisin said, looking for a place to sit.

"Good," Sin-Sin said.

"Fine."

Raisin found a spot on the ground in front of a tree and sat down. Sin-Sin turned his back and started listening again. After a while, he didn't have to turn around to know Raisin was crying.

"What's wrong with you?"

"Nuthin," she sniffled.

"Nuthin?"

They continued to sit in silence.

"My mama come back for me," Raisin finally said.

"She gonna take you away from here?"

"I don't know what that woman gonna do," she said.

"You don't look glad."

"She crazier than you."

"How you mean?" Sin-Sin asked.

"She crazy, that's all."

"Why you think she's crazy?"

"Cause of things she say and do," Raisin said.

"What things?" Sin-Sin asked.

"She didn't come to her own mama's funeral," she said, shaking her head like she'd seen Miss Marius do.

"So? Maybe she was sick or something," Sin-Sin said.

Raisin shrugged her shoulders and hung her head on her chest. Sin-Sin had to strain to catch her words.

"And she say a dead man messing with me."

"Huh?"

She kept mumbling, "He dead a hundred years . . . "

"Who?"

"My daddy."

Neither one of them said a word now. Sin-Sin looked up into the trees, away from the pain in Raisin's face.

"That what she come back for. Not me. She come back for him," Raisin said.

"Your daddy?"

"That's what she say."

"How'd he die?"

Raisin looked like she didn't want to say.

"She say he just laid down and died. Buried hisself in a hole in the woods and made his soul walk away."

"Like them old Africans Blue talks about?" Sin-Sin asked.

"How I'm gonna know? That's what she say," Raisin said.

"Why is he coming around messing with you?" Sin-Sin asked.

"I don't know. All I know is I don't want no parts of him or her."

"What's he coming for you for, though?"

"She say his spirit can't rest. Cause of the way he died and all."

"The burying?" Sin-Sin asked.

Raisin nodded her head.

"She say ain't none of us supposed to go like that. Say our souls won't never find peace. She say we got to help him rest, got to help his spirit find peace."

"I bet Blue can help you and your mama."

"She ain't my mama," Raisin said, drawing her hand up into a fist.

"Well, whoever she is, he can help," Sin-Sin said.

"What give her the right to come and turn everything every whichaway?"

"Mamas always do that kind of stuff," Sin-Sin said.

"Coming around here talking about taking me back to Chicago," Raisin went on.

"Chicago's a long way from here," Sin-Sin said.

"I'm gonna tell her I ain't going."

"We gotta go talk to Blue."

"I ain't going nowhere."

"What're you scared of?"

"Same thing got you sitting out here in the woods by yourself," Raisin said.

"I ain't scared of Blue," Sin-Sin said as he stood and brushed off his pants. He turned and gave Raisin a stony look as she stood and stalked off through the trees.

I I I

▼

S IN-SIN WAS SORRY to see Raisin go. He would've liked to help
her, but didn't really know . . .

He could help Raisin.

He sat back down under a tree whose leaves were starting to
change color. Green leaking out like blood from a body, one dark
body, turning soft and pale.

He closed his eyes and thought about Raisin. Thought about
the smallness of her, the softness beneath her wrinkled skin. He
thought about her lips against his, the tongue water in her
mouth. A curious pleasure rose from his toes and crept up his
legs. He shook his head, jiggled his body. He was not here for this
hardness. He needed to figure out how to help a friend.

He opened his eyes and looked deep into his hand-eye, as far
into the core of Raisin as he could look in order to feel her mother.

* * *

Red. Black. Old blue-black. New red running. Waves. A burning swirl of water. At the bottom, the hot sea-bottom, a child. Floating. Pulsing inside a sack without sound. Farther back, a girl still smelling of her mother's milk, rounding. Spilling forth with light. Something like a shadow moves around her, seeps inside her, glows. She knows no mother's love. Knows no mother's love. She is lost, adrift in the radiance of her shadow-lover. He holds her against a tree. She holds him against a tree. Climbs, wraps herself around the trunk. She is gleaming, incandescent in the tree-black night. She pulls light from the shadow, soft watery light. The shadow draws light from her. Long, thirsting, pull.

Sin-Sin stopped his feeling of Raisin's mother. A cold wet finger of air moved along his spine. Blue would've said someone walked across his grave. It was a man-spirit, whispering words Sin-Sin could barely hear, calling out to Raisin like she belonged to him. "Baby girl . . . Baby girl." Sin-Sin looked around him, peered steadily, quietly into the trees. He didn't see anything, hear anyone. And yet he was sure if he wanted to, he could reach behind and wipe wetness from the skin on his back.

Whose voice was getting inside his head?

"You can't put a name on me."

Sin-Sin's head felt heavy. He shook it to clear the roar growing inside.

"You can't shake me loose, less I wanna be shook."

Sin-Sin felt the wetness on his skin again.

"You wanna know about Raisin and her mama and daddy?"

Sin-Sin's eyes closed, though he struggled to keep them open. All around him was water, thick black water. Deep. He was far inside another world. Gasping. Choking. Water flowing through his nose like air. The more his legs fought the wetness, the further he sank. Into a bottomless pitch, the black at the beginning of the world.

*   *   *

"Some things you gotta leave alone, boy," Blue told him later. "There's things you ain't ready for, got no idea how to handle.

"You wanna know about *your* daddy?" Blue asked.

Sin-Sin thought of the tests he had passed so Blue would think he was ready to know his manhood and would willingly give him his own knife.

"You gotta be able to keep standing, boy," Blue had said. "No matter how rough it get, no matter how many times life knock you down. You gotta get back up on your feet. That's what's gonna make you a man."

He did not question Blue. Not the time he had to stand in the woods in the same position, the same place, all day and way into the night. Not the first time Blue had told him he needed to make himself pure and had given him the hateful yellow brew in the black wooden bowl to drink.

"To help you learn how to see inside yourself," Blue had said.

Sin-Sin had not questioned Blue when Blue brushed his body with wide green leaves that came from a tree Sin-Sin had never seen before. Not when he had to lay in the woods on a mat all night and stay awake watching the blinking, fading stars. He had never questioned Blue.

More than anything, now, especially now, Sin-Sin wanted to be a man. He wanted to know about his daddy.

But it was getting so he didn't know if things he was feeling were real things, or dreams. The faceless man inside the orange cloud who had visited his mother, the voices inside his head. Was that real?

"Your body. Listen to your body," Blue had told him. "It's how we come to remember. Your body holds the memories inside. Inside, where can't nobody see. But I see and I know.

"What happened to my daddy ain't no different from what happened to yours. All of ours. Same thing happened to our mamas, but in a different way. Things in life'll wear on you. Push you till your strong parts get weak. Get you wanting to give up every last piece of yourself. Once you lose yourself, you lose your soul.

"All they need is one little hole, just one crack, and the soulcatcher's in. Once they catch your soul, it's gone. The soul gets confused and can't find its way back cause of all the confusion inside you and all around in the world. Get you so you change your ways and ain't the same somebody the soul come back looking for.

"Yeah, my daddy went down in the water, plenty folks around here did. What else could we do, what would you do somebody try to take away the Ones who made your world, your ways, your name, your very self and try to turn you into something not human?"

Blue looked deep inside Sin-Sin. He sighed and said, "You gotta know other folks' stories to find your own. Here's mine, I'm passing it to you cause your daddy can't, like my daddy didn't. It's yours now, too. If you take it, no soulcatcher can steal our story again."

Soulcatcher

I

Blue

▼

WHEN BLUE WAS FOURTEEN he met an old man, Mr. Goodnight. Blue was mute from bearing the weight of his mother's silence and his own shame. He had not avenged his father's murder, and helplessness had flooded him till he felt he was drowning in a pit of rage.

"The boy will talk when he got something to say," Mr. Goodnight had told Blue's mother when they went to get Blue's few precious things. "Sometimes things happen and we just ain't got no words. Sides, this boy don't learn something to do with his mind, he end up hanging from a tree somewhere. I'll learn him something, or nuther."

His mother hugged Blue for the first time since his daddy died.

"You gonna be a man now, Blue. Your daddy would've wanted it. You old enough to know there's things won't none of us ever understand."

The warmth from his mama's body touched the knot inside Blue. A scream began to build and move inside his chest like a lead bubble stretching and swelling his ribs.

"You couldn't save him, Blue. Wasn't nuthin for you to do."

Blue held his roar inside.

His mother had held him for a long time, like he was seven again and nothing had come between them, like he could again find comfort in her warm cotton skirt, like she knew she would not see him again.

"I thank you, Mr. Goodnight," was the last thing Blue had heard her say, and then she was gone.

I I

THE OLD MAN TOOK BLUE into the one-room shack he called home way back up in the woods. The old man slept on a low wood bed in one corner of the room, while Blue slept on a pallet on the smooth dirt floor. His pallet was next to high shelves holding dusty bottles of dark liquids and light-colored powders in short glass jars.

A thin screen divided the room they slept in from the back corner of the house, where a gray-smeared icebox and lopsided white stove stood.

The one window in the house was streaked green. The house smelled like wet dirt.

"All I need's right here, boy. Got my fish and my garden and a piece of myself. Don't need nuthin sides this."

The old man talked like he was older than anybody Blue had ever seen, but his luminous skin was a smooth-fitting mask over his dark face. He had reddish-orange hair. Sometimes it seemed like an orange halo surrounded the old man's body.

He kept his teeth in a glass on the floor by his bed. Big square sandpapery-feeling yellowish teeth that looked like they were made out of the same wood used to build the house. He hated putting those teeth in his mouth.

"Feel like a hoss when I got these in," he'd always say, grumbling.

Blue's days continued to pass in silence. The old man didn't pay him much attention. He'd yammer to himself sometimes, and others, he'd be quiet as Blue.

"What you know about plants, boy?" he asked after a week of Blue's silent company.

Blue closed his eyes and ducked his head.

"You sure? You ain't never had no dream about roots?"

Blue nodded, then shook his head.

"Well, I'm gonna teach you the little bit I know. Got my learning from dreams. Ever since I was about your age, I could go to sleep sick and dream how to get well. Dreams fixed all kind of sickness. Mine and other folks. All kind of power in plants and dreams. Good and bad. You need to learn about the bad first, so you can preciate the good."

Blue acted like he didn't care nuthin about plants or nuthin else.

"Well, you got the right attitude," the old man said, laughing.

Blue sat still as a stone.

"That's a joke. Ain't you never heard one before? You s'posed to laugh. You can laugh, can't you?"

Blue stared into the old man's dead-leaf eyes. The old man shook his head and sighed.

"You like looking in a mirror, boy. Come on."

Blue clumped behind the old man on needle-laced paths

through the trees, his halfhearted steps mocking other soundless ones.

"Some we got to wait till dark to get. We'll dig awhile for the roots I need. Look careful. I want you to see how you can tell how old these plants are by the scars on their roots. See, we all got scars, boy. We all got em. Some sitting on the outside, others way down, deep down. Ain't no sin in having em. Scars learn us what this life-thing's about. Make us real. Not trying to heal a scar's the sin."

The old man's words made a heaviness fall on Blue. He followed him, then sat on the ground still as a stone, watching but not seeing as the old man pulled roots from the ground and picked leaves off plants he said was magic.

"Sometimes quiet a way to wound yourself, boy," the old man said haltingly. "A funny kinda way of dying slow."

Blue's bones felt as if they were falling in on themselves from the weight of the silence he'd been carrying inside. The old man kept pulling and picking, oblivious to the cracking inside Blue.

Blue wanted to run but didn't, wanted to hold on to the shield of his silence, and yet, the slow chanting voice of the old man made him want to bury his quiet in the soft dusky earth.

"Many a time we think we out here in the world alone, but we ain't. Think don't nobody know about our sufferation. But there's them that know and feel our hurt right along with us. That might not be no sweet in your sour, but it always rest my mind a bit."

Blue looked the old man in his tawny-orange–colored eyes for the first time. There was no judgment in his eyes. No mocking. No betrayal. Only a misty yellow-orange light, two warm streams of kindness watching him.

I I I

▼

WHAT I'M TEACHING YOU, boy, go back a long way, all the way back to old Africa. You gonna haveta hold it in your mind till it get to be a part of your body, it just there."

The old man pulled a vial of yellow liquid from the pocket of his jacket, and drank.

Blue sat on a small quilt of rusty-colored pine needles and rested the tight bundle inside himself.

The old man sat for a while as the liquid quieted his mind. He closed his eyes, then spoke as if from the depths of a dream.

"We was happy then. Before the breaking, before the pale darkness, before our souls run from our bodies in buck-naked terror, we was free.

"People with wings, we could fly then. Soft yielding earth give us food then. Animals, plants was kin then. Rivers moving easy as good blood give us water, water pure as light in a star.

"We feed the earth then. Love her and give her food then. Food that been blessed by the gods.

"The gods hear our cries then. When we moan. When we beseech the good earth, the gods hear our cries.

"We touch the gods with trembly hands then. Kiss them with shaky lips then. The gods walked the soft road with us here then, when the earth was good.

"We turned from the earth then. Turned from the earth and the animals then. Turned from the plants and the rivers then.

"Full of ourselves, we was lowly then. Thought we could cut up the earth then. Thought we could keep pieces of the earth in our pockets then. Call her our own then.

"Thought this one different from that one then. Thought this one better than that one then. Thought this one less than that one then. Thought ourselves mighty then. Strong enough to rule over all the world then.

"Full of ourselves, we was low then. Men full, commanded women full, who ruled the children full then. Elders walked the earth confused then. Elders held the old words in their heads full then. Ancestors waited for the old words from the elders then, to give to the gods then. To try to help us then. To try to talk to the gods for us then. Elders held the old words in their heads full then.

"The gods took out their swords then. The gods cut us with their swords then. The gods stopped their ears then. The gods turned from us when we were full and the earth was empty then.

"The gods called our souls away from us then. Turned away from us and took our souls then. Took our wings then. Took our soft light and laughter then. Took our world and all we loved then, because we got fat and didn't feed her then.

"Thousands of seasons passed. Then the cold darkness came. The white-fingered shadow came. The thousand-yeared pale darkness came. The floating colorless phantom came. The bone ships of bleached darkness came. The chalky ghost came. The bitter ashy darkness came. A darkness new to our world came. A pearly-toothed pale darkness came and chomped on our spirits like they was small white bones.

"Now our souls are walking in the other world. Confused, they keep on walking. Disgusted, they keep on walking. Lost, they keep on walking. Moaning, they keep on walking. Walking in the other world. Moaning in the other world cause they don't know where we are."

I V

▼

THE OLD MAN STOPPED HIS DREAM TALK, then cocked his head. "You hear that?"

Blue nodded. He heard the wind whistling through the trees.

"They trying to get back to our bodies, but we got to learn how to listen. Got to help em get back by healing the wounds to our spirits."

Blue looked away from the old man's tears. His daddy was the only man he had ever seen cry, and he'd only seen him cry that one bitter time.

"We best get on back home. Got what I come for."

A small piece of sound fell away from the ball of silence inside Blue and moved in his body like a rusty chain as he slowly followed the old man.

"Arrgh," was the only sound he was able to push out of his lips.

The old man turned and looked at Blue.

"It's all right, son. We got plenty time," he said, resuming his steady pace toward home.

Blue watched the back of the old man's brown coat brush against his thin legs as he walked. He let the rusty air out of his lungs seven more times before they reached the mustardseed plants next to the front step of the old man's house.

"Boy, anybody ever tell you you sound like a old floor squeaking?" The old man laughed as he passed under the dung-covered horseshoe nailed over the only door in his house.

Later that night, after the old man had soaked his feet in a white bowl of water sprinkled with garlic, thyme, dry basil leaves, parsley flakes, sage, and saltpeter and had rubbed himself down with bay rum, he handed Blue a small red flannel sack with pieces of garlic inside.

Blue wrinkled his nose and shook his head, no.

"Wear this around your neck, boy. It protect you good as silence."

Slowly, surely, Blue began to talk again. Not much. He would never be one to run his mouth like a bucket with a hole in it, but he was able to speak, able to learn how to talk with the old man.

V

▼

B LUE STAYED WITH THE OLD MAN seven years, learning his strange
old ways.

"What got you scared, boy?" the old man asked one slow day.

"I keep seeing pictures," Blue said slowly. "Things I don't
wanna see when I open my eyes."

"Close your eyes and tell it," the old man said.

The old man looked at Blue, those orange eyes full of bright
mist that moved to reach out to Blue without touching him.

"It's your story, son. You the only one can tell it. It's time."

Blue laid in the bed and closed his eyes. He took a deep rattling breath.

"I see my daddy drowning. I see my mama drowning too,
but in silence. I see me standing with my hands tied, not trying
to help, not even knowing how. I can't get the picture out of my
mind."

"Maybe it supposed to stay, then. Tell it."

"I don't wanna remember."

"But you gotta. Gotta go down in that hurting place fore you be all right. "

"I see things . . . remember my daddy crying. Never saw him cry before. Never saw no man cry before. I felt scared then. My daddy was crying. Loud, slobbering crying. Mama was holding herself still. Didn't want none of us to know what was happening. But I heard him, and I went to him thinking somehow I could make it all right, ease those tired lines in the black of his skin . . . 'I can't tell you what I need now, son,' all he say while he keep on crying. Heard mama whisper, 'They coming?' And daddy cold, 'What you think?' . . . member him holding a heavy rock in his hands. And I say, 'Daddy?' And that all I say, mama say, 'Hush now. Go on back in your room and sit. Be still. We all just need to be still.' Mama's whispers were hot. Her hands were hot, patting, trying to soothe what couldn't, what wouldn't ever be soothed or made right . . .

"The click-thump of horses on the road, the way the night air slapped me when daddy opened the door and ran out in the yard. The light from the lanterns was brilliant around him, and the light ran along the length of the whip when it was raised in the air. The whip beat the air like strange whooshing music and hit my daddy's back like a wet drumbeat while he danced, a black frame of light in the circle of snorting, sweating horses.

"He broke out of the circle, ran down the road . . . the horses behind . . . chasing my daddy down in that river's cool embrace . . . he dance-step in the water . . . he stand for a minute, still, so still. He turn back to the muddy bank and I think he looking for something, somebody. Maybe he looking for me. He don't see me, though, don't none of em see me. He see ain't nobody there, then his body go down, long arms slapping that fast white water. That was the only time I ever saw fear on his face, when the water took him down down down."

"Didn't none of us know how to swim back then, boy. Didn't none of us know how to hold on to our breath and believe. Believe we could remember, remember what we always knew. The river was the line, boy. The line they used to keep us from flying, from being free. Told us there was things under that water worse than chains. And most of us believed em."

"But I didn't do nuthin, just watched em run him into that river."

"Your mama told you you didn't have nuthin to do with that evil."

The old man already knew about the white man who had come and pushed his mother down in the red dirt and put his yellow teeth to her breast, his tongue between her legs. He knew Blue's mother couldn't get away from the man, couldn't raise her hand to a white man, any white man.

"All of our skins broke open from her wounds, all of us felt the violation. All the way back to the Old Ones. Your daddy felt the wounds as deep and sharp as your mama. And the only way we knew how much she felt was by the quiet that come and grabbed her soul. That the kind of pain don't move, it just stay long and deep inside. Can't nobody ease the hush of that hurt away."

Blue was silent.

"Your trouble is you act like you past saving, past redemption," the old man said, shaking his head like a doctor with bad news.

"But what I'm supposed to do?"

"You supposed to hold what happened inside till it make some kinda sense, then you gonna make sure it don't happen again. Not ever again."

"How I'm gonna do that?"

"What you do gonna be different from your daddy. He kilt the man who hurt your mama and he burned the hanging tree down. We all gets one chance to turn things back around. You gonna get your chance. Your bones'll tell you when your chance come."

"Mama tried to protect him."

"They was both all the protection they thought they had. All what was left for your daddy to do was what he do and fix that tree."

"They woulda strung him up like all the others," Blue said.

"You know they woulda, son. And your daddy knew it, too, but he wasn't gonna let em have the satisfaction."

"That man never shoulda put his hands on mama."

"He know that now, but then he thinking colored women like a fielda black dirt he can break open and turn over, some wild kinda tree he got the right to cut down."

"Mama said it wasn't nuthin. It didn't mean nuthin."

"Your mama didn't want your daddy to go out and get kilt. She didn't understand that her saying that was the same as telling your daddy his whole world wasn't nuthin, and they both knew that wasn't true. Your daddy was lucky. He went the way he wanted to go."

"But he wasn't ready. He was scared of that water."

"He was ready as he could ever be, boy. If he wasn't, he wouldn'ta never set a torch to that tree. It does something to you when you look on evil and don't try to make it right. Your daddy walked by that tree many a day in his life, plenty days he walked by and seen men hanging in the branches like broken-limbed berries."

V I

▼

A S BLUE LIVED WITH THE OLD MAN, he learned his secrets about plants, the way they talk and heal. Ways they can hurt.

One day, soon after Blue's twenty-first birthday, when he'd been spending a lot of time at the house of a chocolate drop of a girl named Marius, he went to the old man with a strange request.

"Marius say she gonna marry Nathan."

"What's that you say?" the old man asked, barely able to hear now.

"I say Marius say she gonna marry Nathan on accounta he know how to work land and all she say I know how to work is roots."

"That right?"

"I tell her I don't know nuthin about working no roots, but she scared and don't believe me since I been living out here with you all this time."

"Hmm," was all the old man said.

Blue acted like he was straightening up the shelf where the old man kept his herbs and things in bottles and jars.

"She say you know about wanga, black magic."

"That right?" The old man closed his eyes to go back to sleep.

"Do you?"

"Do I what?"

"Know how to put a bad spell on folks?"

The old man was quiet for so long Blue thought he had gone to sleep.

"Use whatever I got gainst those who hurt me or mine. What you think? You think I'ma be out in this world without no protection, walking around madmen and murderers and not be able to defend myself? What kind of fool you take me for, boy?" The old man was getting more and more agitated.

"Haven't I learned you nuthin in all these years? Ain't you been listening to a thing I ever told you? I'ma go outta here using my last breath to do work gainst those what tried to steal my soul. Humph. If you had any sense you'd be doing the same steada chasing behind that wide-tailed gal."

"I been thinking it's time I find me a wife to take up with."

"Ain't never had no woman living out here. Done learned how to feel peace inside myself all by myself. You know we all gotta learn how to be alone, boy. And at the very end we all gotta leave here alone."

"I ain't saying I'd bring her out here, just saying I need to find me a wife."

The old man's heavy breathing was the only sound in the room.

"Always thought I'd be the first one to go," he said heavily.

"Now you know I ain't gonna stay out here and live offa you forever."

"We living off each other, not one off the other. But you right. Every coming together ends in a pulling apart. It's a good thing you talking about doing. We all gots to feed and be fed. When I'm gone, you'll feed me. But who's gonna feed you? We can't never break the line, boy. Not never."

"I need a wanga for Nathan."

"What? You don't wanna work no bad magic on nobody less you ready for the bad to come back on you, or you wanna do work gainst the ones who tried to steal our souls."

"I don't wanna hurt him. I just wanna stop him from bothering Marius, making her think she could have a good life with him, stead of me."

"Maybe she right. You can't be the judge on that."

"You gonna help me or Nathan?" Blue asked, sticking out his chest.

The old man looked at him and shook his head.

"I see you done got a whiffa that gal and you ain't gonna listen to nobody talking sense. I'll have something for you tomorrow."

The next day the old man handed Blue a red flannel bag.

Blue sniffed at it.

"Red pepper?"

The old man nodded his head.

"Toss this in the path of Nathan and Marius. It won't hurt em, but it sure will make em fuss and fight."

"What is it?"

"It's what you asked for."

Blue caressed the soft-skinned bag.

"I'm finally gonna get to be a man," he said, smiling.

"Rubbing up next to some gal ain't gonna make you a man. It's the head, boy. The best part of your soul sitting right inside your head. That's where your old guardian sit, ancestor older, got as much power as the gods. That's where all your gold is, boy. All your power and glory. Sitting right inside your head. Your head's gonna make you into a man, not that gal."

Blue thought about what the old man said the next time he saw Marius and Nathan standing together, smiling. He itched to follow them and throw the charm at their slow dragging feet, but he didn't. The thought of Nathan holding Marius's warm strong body made Blue feel small inside. A little voice in his head told him to go ahead and throw the charm, but instead of throwing it at the two lovers, he tossed it deep inside a thick green bush as he walked home to the old man.

"Get your gal?" the old man asked grumpily.

"She wasn't never my gal," was all Blue said as he laid down on his pallet and closed his eyes.

Several months later the old man was dead sick. He lay in the narrow bed and mist hung over his body.

"Don't go around looking like that, ain't none of us long for this world, boy. This old body just skin and bones. I'm gonna live on inside you."

"I know how to make you well," Blue said, grabbing the root bag and heading out the door.

"Ain't nuthin for this but a pine box, boy. Ain't none of us quick enough to snatch ourselves out of the hands of death. Seem like it take most your life to get quick enough to turn around and catch what's good inside youself, that's when you wake up. Then you turn around and the gods is calling you. Once they call, you gotta go."

"I ain't ready for you to go," Blue said, tightening inside.

"You ain't got no say-so. Not in this, boy. But you ready. Ready to stand up for yourself and be a man. You thought they took something from you when they kilt your daddy and they did, but your daddy left you a something when he went. I could see it in your eyes, boy, way back when I took you from your mama, and you didn't even haveta say a word, but I knew. You a laster, boy. You a tough somebody what's gonna hold on, to the old ways, to our memories, to our gods. Ain't nuthin worse than a fool ain't got sense enough to hold on to they gods. You gotta remember the ones who went before you and the ones coming after you, they who you coming to be, they who we all gonna be."

VII

▼

THE OLD MAN TALKING LOW WHISPERS. Singing, telling stories with sounds, making Blue forget hisself, his own sorrow, his mama and daddy, the blacks and whites of all their fears.

The old man laying in his bed sweating, that orange mist swirling around like a hurricane and he was inside the eye. He was saying words Blue never heard fall out of nobody's mouth, not even in dreams.

The sounds closest to the old man's words that Blue could remember were from the one time his mama took him to a Pentecostal church. There he heard the rising falling sinking swimming words pushing out of the preacher's chest and falling into one poor soul's empty heart. One cold heart waiting for the precise sounds rising and falling from the black and white keys of the box piano and swirling in the white-black air electric with sound. Sound falling into some body, one twisting turning dark body, once hollow, now filling with the preacher's whining rising pitch.

The turn of the piano's sweet licks filled the hollow, the long dark void inside that one twisting turning body, the body that fell out in the floor, and Blue heard the same sounds from the old man now, luminous silky black sounds, older than old, falling from out of the old man's mouth, "Talking to Africa, boy. Straight line home," the last words said, the last sounds Blue was able to make out.

VIII

▼

L ONG AFTER THE OLD MAN WAS GONE, Blue saw Sin-Sin standing
off to himself in town. A trail of orange mist circled the boy's
head like a dust devil. A question shot straight at him from the
eyes of the boy into his own stilled heart, where it pulsed like a
broken-down drumbeat: "Who's gonna love you? Who's gonna
love you now, now, now? . . . "

Blue's bones clicked when he saw Sin-Sin, twenty-one years
after the old man's death. The click traveled from the shells of his
ankles to his kneecaps and then up each knot of his spine until
he felt himself shaking in his hard places, in his broken places,
shaking and clicking like a rattle.

He could hear the old man whisper, "Turn-around time,"
when he looked into Sin-Sin's eyes and saw the fear inside, wet as
his own.

Sin-Sin made him think about silence. Water and silence. A

watery veil of quiet no hands could ever reach through. Deep quiet. Old quiet. A screaming quiet that once had pierced Blue's body and held him tight as a tomb.

Sin-Sin made Blue reach through the veil, made him reach and grab and take a strong hold.

The same silence in Sin-Sin touched Blue, made him want to hold Sin-Sin like he'd never been able to hold himself, like Blue wished he could've grabbed hold of his own father when his father slipped through the water of the river.

The familiar silence and mist surrounding the boy called out to Blue, made him draw near, bound him to Sin-Sin like he'd never been bound to anyone else.

Blue knew he couldn't be quiet anymore, knew he was going to open his mouth and tell Sin-Sin the old man's words. Couldn't Blue be a father to Sin-Sin, the way Mr. Goodnight was Blue's own spirit-father? All the things Mr. Goodnight had taught Blue—the secrets about plants, the blood memories, the wanga—all the things Blue had thought he'd forgotten after holding them inside so long, all the buried, battered words began to rush inside his head like old souls on a dark road to a new blue world. He had to give the words to Sin-Sin.

"We can't never break the line, boy. Not never," the old man had often said.

The line. From the river holding the spirit of his daddy to the death of his mama from a cancer that ate her soul. From the old man's words about the gods, to Blue's own plant-holding hands, to the quiet orange soul of the boy.

After seeing the boy, Blue knew the old man's words had walked a sure but crooked-line circle.

"We can't never break the line."

Blue would tell Sin-Sin these things and more when he came to him out in the woods.

SECTION 8

One Dark Body

I

Raisin

▼

WISH THESE STICKS crackling up under my feet was Sin-Sin's bones. Ain't never gonna take up for him no more, crazy orange boy. Talking about being a man and scared to death of Blue. Stupid boy. Dumb trying-to-be-a-man boy. Scaredy boy. What kind of man he gonna be?

"You looking for me?"

Stop walking and turn my head to the trees. Look straight in the shine of Blue's neckbeads.

"Huh?"

"You out here looking for me?" Blue asked.

"I'm on my way home."

"To your mama?" he ask, grinning.

Don't like his questions or the smiley look in his eyes, like he know me when he don't. Don't say nuthin. Let him see he can't talk to me like he do that crazy boy.

"Some folks would be glad they mama come for em," he say.

"Some folks would," I say.

His teeth big and white and shiny. He laugh like he got a choke stuck in his throat.

"Sin-Sin's back up the way. Guess you getting ready to turn him into a man," I say, scratching my feet in the ground.

He don't say nuthin. Act like he supposed to be the one doing all the asking.

"I ain't looking for Sin-Sin," he say.

She send him. I know she do. Nobody else fretting with my life like a dog worrying a bone.

"What you want with me?" I finally ask.

"What YOU want with ME?" he ask.

He act about crazy as Nola Barnett. Why do crazy people turn they talk all upside-turned-around? Bet you a quarter them beads and shells ain't even wanga.

"Don't want nuthin. Just on my way home," I say.

"Walking here and you don't want nuthin with me?" he ask.

"These ain't yours," I say, spreading my arms to the trees.

Don't like the way he keeps looking at me, don't like the way he keep looking through me, inside and around me, under my skin and over my bones like blood.

"You better come with me," he say.

"Huh?"

"Got something for your mama, you better come get it."

"Why can't she get it herself?" I ask.

"Cause you gonna get it for her," he say.

Look inside black black. The smooth stone hanging around his neck. His eyes, two holes full of dark water. He don't say nuthin. I don't say nuthin. Pick my feet up and follow. Quickly, softly through the trees.

I I

▼

WE WALK ALMOST TO THE LAKE before we get to Blue's gray shack leaning up against that twisted double-trunk yellow-tipped tree. It quiet out here. Don't hear nuthin but my feet dragging cross the ground. Blue don't make no noise here or out in the woods. He all the time walking around hushed as death.

"You can come in here, ain't got no plans to hurt you," he say, walking inside the door.

Not going in there, gonna wait right here and get what I'm supposed to get. But he turn around, and that glassy stone around his neck blink like a see-through eye, and tell me to go in, so I do.

It green dark in here. Green dark and smell like wet trees.

"I got all the light I need inside me," Blue say, like he know what I'm thinking, while he grunt and rummage through dusty bottles on a shelf.

I stay by the door. Don't care what that rock act like it telling me to do.

"You go to school. You ever see all the bad things they say about darkness in them books?"

I shake my head cause I don't want him to start talking like no Bible and have this take longer than it have to.

"Well, I did," he say. "Read about it one time in a book supposed to have the meaning of things inside. Looked up black and what it say? Dirty. Evil. Wicked. Sad. No light." He stop his rustling and look at me hard-like.

"I look like any of them things to you?"

Shake my head no. My hand almost touch the top of a coon skull sitting on a table by the door.

He keep picking up bottles and putting em down and grunting, all the while he talking to me. See some smaller skulls sitting on the shelf mixed in with them dusty bottles.

He find what he looking for, then stand still. He look at me and laugh.

"Watch out. White people don't know what they talking about. Don't want you to know nuthin about yourself. All you come out of is black, girl, pure dark. The beginning, the end, all black. Don't you forget it, neither. Them folks'll have your mind so turned around, you'll be thinking crazy as them. But you look at all this light in me. Look. You got the same in you. Give this to your mama, I told her what to do."

He hand me a little red box with squiggly lines carved in the leather.

"This from your daddy's grave."

I almost drop the box on his bare wood floor.

"Careful, now. You old enough to know," all he say when he wave me off back in the trees.

I I I

Nola

▼

As Nola lay on the quilt-covered bed, she knew her days of waiting to put El to rest were coming to an end. Soon his bones could be still.

Light slid over her body in wide-slatted bars. She heard the soft-throated call of doves blessing the woods, the long honking laughter of black-necked geese, the muted peeps of other gentle praising birds.

She smoothed the shell of her body, which softened like dark cloth under the iron of her hands.

She felt all the days of her life in Pearl sitting like a low-slung sun inside her belly, turning the water inside her mouth pickley hot.

The room filled with memories smelling of red cedar and sage, a dry, burning, man's smell. El.

She closed her eyes, took a long breath and eased his heavy

scent inside her body as if she were again learning who he was. The pure, sure lines of his nose, the soft black mat of hair covering his cheeks and chin, the full lips that opened like a strongbox of dark hope.

She remembered the day in the woods when she had leaned against a soft-barked tree and pulled El close to her slowly swelling body. Remembered the smell of hot foliage, remembered her hands holding the domes of his shoulders underneath his shirt, the slow drag of fingertips across the rising island of flesh that was his birthmark.

She had rested her body on El. Laid the weight of her life at their feet, closed her eyes and rested.

Nola remembered the stern face of Ouida Barnett rising out of the darkness of her mind, a curious gleam in her eyes.

Nola had turned from her mother's frowning face shining before her eyes. Ouida Barnett's eyes bright with the light of disappointment, that bitter, wounding colored woman's disease.

Nola had packed the image of her mother away in a tight white box, back in a musty corner of her mind, as she slowly unbuttoned El's shirt.

The sight of his smooth black skin made her mouth water. She had been thirsting for love so long in her mother's house.

Nola drew her tongue over El's body until his skin began to liquefy.

She unbuttoned his blue jeans and slid them, over high round buttocks, down to his ankles.

She held his penis, swaying before her, lightly in her hands. She dropped and knelt on pine needles and leaves broken on the ground and took him into her mouth.

Her body swayed to the beat of El's frenzied rocking and moans until her tingling lips drew a cord of liquid pulsing light from inside him.

He had knelt before her then.

Dropped to his knees on the leaf-implanted ground and stroked her naked legs.

His lips brushed the insides of her knees and calves, before moving higher to the delicate flesh of her thighs, where he nibbled her skin until she hummed with pleasure.

Nola had pulled El's head to that part of her belly she could not see, but could feel, burning now, yearning for fusion, wanting the plunge of his sweet searching tongue.

The gentleness of his hands had unnerved her, as he caressed the dark rising beneath her dress like a waxing moon; each stroke, each circling of fingertips on her skin made her feel as if he were sculpting her and the baby out of the clay of their awaiting life together.

This was not the love of her mother, Ouida Barnett. Not a long seeking of self in other selves, not a great yawning gap of waiting empty.

This was not the curious love of her father, not the dull appreciation in his hypnotic, narcotic eyes.

The love she felt for El was a circle, a ring, a world; something that sprang from itself, full, spinning, free. A love as bright with darkness as a black hole dense with stars.

This was a feeling she thought she could grasp in her strong young arms and hold onto, something elusively solid, something real.

She remembered El talking about wanting to leave his body, El always telling her he really knew how. She had never believed him.

"The old folks know how. Them folks come over on them slave ships knew how. Some of em did it. Just laid down and was still. Let their souls walk away from their bodies till all that was left was the bones."

"You supposed to be here. You better keep both your feet on this ground. Don't quit on me."

"Something calling me, Nola. I can feel it calling."

"This your home, El. Our child right here in this world. In this belly. This one. Feel this."

El had ignored the gift of the belly she offered and kept on staring like he was looking on some other shining motionless world.

"You ever feel something pulling you, something liquid, gentle, sweet?"

"Not like you talking about. This our life. These my hands holding you."

"Something strong . . . "

"My love strong."

"Quiet. Whispery watery quiet. Peace."

"We'll make us a quiet place, find us a peaceful place in this world."

"I'm tired, Nola."

"You tired? You too young to be tired. You ain't even carrying the baby."

"But I'll be carrying that baby once it comes. I'm gonna haveta carry the load. Gonna get packed like a mule."

"We both gonna work."

"But I'm gonna haveta go down in them mines. Just like my daddy and all the other men around here. That's the only kinda work a colored man can do. Go down in a hole and dig. Get turned into some kinda sad sorry machine. Ain't you ever noticed how none of em talk about what it's like? Don't say nuthin about what it does to you going down into a hole every day. But I can see it, Nola. Even if they don't say. Living gonna suck on my life till ain't nuthin left but light behind soft black bones."

"What about the good in life, El? Me and the baby. Love? You know how your people think. How they say taking your own life's the same thing as murder. It ain't right. Your spirit won't ever find peace. They don't believe in nuthin like that."

"I can't carry you and the baby and what-all my people think the rest of my life. Ain't never gonna be free."

Nola felt the band breaking, saw the dull glow of a crumbling ring, smelled the circle make a slow rusty turn.

"We your people now, El. The baby and me. We could always work a while, then leave. Start over somplace else."

"Can't do it, Nola. I don't think I can go down in that hole and stay alive. Not here or noplace. That hole would be waiting on me anyplace else I'd go. Can't do it. Not for you. Not for nobody."

"Your people don't hold no stock in you trying to leave here and not coming back, El. Nuthin good gonna ever come from doing something like that. You won't never get no rest you do something like that, El. Not never. That's one of the worst things your people say you can do."

"Nobody gonna turn me into no shadow."

"We all tired, El. We all gonna be tired long as we keep living. Don't you see? We all gotta put our feet on this ground and grab hold of this life tight as we can. We ain't got no choice but to hold on. Make the best outta what we got. Try to do a good thing while we here. It ain't too much to ask. Ask your people what happen when you just let go."

Nola hadn't believed El was serious. She had hoped he was talking to hear himself talk. But El did not ask his people anything, he had simply opened his arms and let go. They found his body in a shallow grave he had dug for himself out in the woods, wrapped inside a dirt-covered white sheet, once-strong arms, floppy on his chest, not far from the long-legged tree where he and Nola had often made love.

I V

▼

NOLA HAD LEFT HER BODY THEN. Sucked into the middle of fast, furious winds, she floated inside the eye of herself, a great white eye inside herself, where she found a still place, a sharp white place, where nothing moved.

Nola lived her life from the center of that stillness, that blinding silent fury, that white unblinking eye.

She remembered walking to the grave El had dug for himself, the spot of tranquility he had longed for, the place where he had willed his soul to walk away from his body and leave him without substance, light or shadow in a hole in the ground, that tight-lipped womb whose dark hold was more lasting than hers.

She had dropped to the ground and pressed her full belly into the soft dark earth.

"Can you hear me, El? Can you hear? I am bringing you

this, bringing you all of me, all that is me, the swelling bowl of my life, like gold, I am bringing you the sun in my heart, a white slip of moon in my grin, bringing you the dark petals of my life, my legs, my crooked yellow toes, I am bringing you my river of laughter, the sharp sea of my sweat when we love, bringing you my rambling tongue, my fat kisses, my one eye that never blinks, I am bringing you my hips that rock, shake, sing, bringing my fists and sharp elbows, my short fingernails, crazy eyebrows, the lashes that will bald when I'm old, the curious world inside my head, I am bringing you, bringing you me, all of me on this platter of earth, your earth, the place you call home, now, honey, sugar, your true love, the place where you find comfort in another's dark arms, I am bringing you this, bringing you all of this . . . "

V

▼

NOLA LET THE MEMORIES settle back down inside her before she rose from the bed. As she walked past the gilt-edged mirror hanging on the wall, she was startled by a glimpse of Ouida Barnett staring back at her in the mirror's reflection.

She was now the woman she had sworn she would never become.

Her mother's obliteration of her very self for Nola's father was no different, no more offensive or self-serving than Nola's choice to annihilate herself and attempt to destroy another young woman now called Raisin, after the death of El.

Nola shook her head and smiled bitterly as she stood at the window overlooking the front yard and watched Raisin slowly walk into it.

For the first time in years, she could actually feel her body, know it was around, beside, beneath her, feel its contours and silhouettes, the slight crevices of its secrets.

She stood on two solid feet, the roots of two sturdy legs. Her breath flowed from her lungs in deep, even waves. She felt the strength of her breasts rising and falling with each breath, breasts that had never nursed young, yet felt now as if they held milk enough for the world.

She rubbed her flat belly gently, firmly, steadily, as if her touch could heal the torn flesh of her mother's belly wounds.

It had taken Nola twelve years, all of Raisin's life, to be able to look back on the life she had left behind in Pearl and ease a painful knowing into her numbed self: "Nola Barnett, all these years, almost half your life, you stayed a flower on a dead man's grave."

V I

Sin-Sin

▼

RAAAARRRR . . .
Sin-Sin opened his eyes. His room filled with the sound of a roaring, charging wind.

He saw the round black heads of the bedpost at his feet, the leaning chest of drawers, the knob glowing on the door of his closet. It was starting to get light.

He turned his head toward the sound, started to call out for his mother, but a thick pad of darkness covered his eyes.

"Don't speak. Don't even say a word. Put your clothes on."

Sin-Sin didn't recognize the low voice ordering him around the room.

Unsteadily, he slipped on coarse jeans, buttoned a shirt with trembly fingers, pushed woolly-socked feet into a pair of worn half boots.

"Come on."

"But, my mama . . . "

"Not a word," the voice growled as Sin-Sin was pushed out of his room. "Your mama know you going."

The man held Sin-Sin's arms behind his back as he propelled Sin-Sin through the curious maze of his once-familiar home and out into the clear beginning morning.

Blue. He had told Sin-Sin to come when he was ready, but in the end he had come for Sin-Sin, ready or not. The voice had said his mother knew, but what was she supposed to know? He opened his mouth to ask where they were going, but a coarse hand tightened over his lips before he could utter a sound.

"Does an infant speak in its mother's womb?" the voice asked roughly.

Sin-Sin slowly shook his head, no.

"You are like that infant. You are something waiting to be born."

The man took his hand from Sin-Sin's mouth.

"If you need to say something during the next three days, you talk to me soft as deer. When your eyes are not covered, you keep them on the ground between your feet. When you are allowed to eat, don't touch the food with your fingers, take it directly with your mouth from my hands like animals and the souls of the dead."

Sin-Sin felt a terrible fear coil itself in his belly, a cool, shiny, sleek fear.

"Our gods are going to kill you soon. You must never tell all you will learn on this journey, this path of the Night People."

Sin-Sin's legs grew wobbly beneath him. He didn't know if he was truly ready to go the way of these ancestors, these Night People. He heard the boomp boomp of something striking the ground. A chanting, roaring sound began again:

Raaaaaroarrr . . .

"The voice of God will give you courage. You cannot stay a boy full of a woman's blood forever."

Sin-Sin was determined he would not show the fear slithering inside him. He straightened his legs and continued walking in front of the rough-voiced man holding his arms, walking inside the soft darkness covering his eyes.

VII

▼

S IN-SIN LAY IN THE WOODS in a deep hole surrounded by white
clay. He was sandwiched between the leaves and branches
covering his body in the hole with his eyes uncovered. His stomach was full and his naked body warm from the crushed ginger
anointing his skin.

He heard a hissing whistle fly from the black of the trees
and a voice say, "You are going into the darkness of the other
world. The Night People will be there."

Soon Sin-Sin fell into a bottomless sleep and dreamed.

The raw bloody smell of something about to be born fills the
air. He feels the crumbling beads of ginger on his skin. Curry
spice simmers on his tongue.

He sees his naked body rise from the branch-covered pit and
walk three slow circuits around the hole.

A man he has never seen approaches slowly from the thick
black trees. His face is a sleek ebony mask. He is dressed like no

one Sin-Sin has ever seen. He is wearing a long brown tunic, with high soft-skinned boots on his feet. He is covered with bones, bells and beads. The ribbons across his chest are wings. On his right shoulder is a large mirror, "for seeing worlds and catching the souls of the dead," he says.

Sin-Sin follows the winged man to the large leafless elm in the center of the clearing. The white dove feathers flutter in a soft wind. The man motions for Sin-Sin to sit at the base of the two trees in the smaller circle of white clay. Sin-Sin sees the blood decorating the bark of the trees. He sits.

"You are going to meet your father," the winged man says. "But you must climb through your head to go."

The man begins to sing in a language Sin-Sin does not know.

"Ey ya woh ye, ey ya woh ye, oh ya ye woh ye . . . "

Sin-Sin feels the winged man's words fly inside his head. He sees himself getting smaller inside his mind's eye. He begins to climb each rich sound like a rung in a ladder inside his head. He reaches the top of his head climbing the "ey ya woh ye's" of the winged man. He is small on top of his head.

Slowly, Sin-Sin opened his eyes.

The trees surrounded him like giants. As if traveling a great distance, he moved from the pit to the foot of the elm in the clearing. The elm with the dancing dove feathers of his dream.

He stepped back. Before him was a great black face carved into the trunk of the elm. A black wooden face that came out of the tree.

All around him the trees whistled and hissed. Their branches touched the ground like ropes of woolly hair. They had yellow eyes that glowed in the dark.

"You must never betray this," they hissed. "It is what our gods brought to us long ago."

Sin-Sin nodded his assent.

The trees began a long whistling chant.

"Our first god, our oldest god is EyeMe. She was already born when nuthin else was. She made herself out of herself. She made the stars and the sun in the heavens.

"She spit out a seed into the First Waters. The seed floated in winter, grew into a sprout in spring, flowered in summer and lost its many-colored leaves in fall. She is the moon who is both man and woman, the moon who shot her life-giving fire into those leaves which became the many different peoples of the earth.

"She is Mother of the living. Mother of the dead. Mother of the sky and earth. We call her the Mother Killer because she gives life and takes it away. She has many breasts.

"A small piece of her lives inside us all.

"EyeMe made grasses, the bush, and towering trees. She made all the animals of the earth. She made the twelve twin ancestor spirits, our first ancestors who we call the Night People, who lived on the earth before death came into the world.

"In the beginning EyeMe told people to come to her for all that they needed. The first people went to her so much she thought they would wear her out with their requests.

"She made a place for herself in a watery heaven away from the first people and only the Night People talk to her now.

"The first people turned against EyeMe because they couldn't get to her, they forgot about her and thought they were bigger than EyeMe. She moved away from us and watched our fall.

"In our turning, in our breaking, in her leaving, we later allowed ourselves to become bones in the belly of the white-fingered beast. The beast wrapped its thin lips around the souls of our people. Wrapped its tongue around the hearts of our people. Closed its throat on the bodies of our people. The great beast swallowed our people whole.

"We twist and turn in its great belly now. We will twist and turn till the beast spits us out.

"We will be new people then. We will be whole people then. Living on the earth again, in peace, in harmony. Respecting the earth again. Caring for each other again. Knowing we are the trees, the birds, the sun.

"We will know the fish is our sister, the stone our brother. Know we are all leaves fallen from the branch of the same great tree again. Know the tribal songs again, sung back in the very first world.

"Did you dream of The Tree?" they asked. Sin-Sin slowly nodded.

"The face in the tree is EyeMe. This tree is the Firstborn, the first plant made by EyeMe, the ancestor of all other plants.

"We are the Night People. The ancestors of your father. Your ancestors. We have come to kill you so you will know us, know your people and yourself."

The trees stopped their whistling lament. The face on the tree withdrew into the trunk, ever-watchful, still proud.

Sin-Sin walked back to the branch-covered hole and climbed inside, the trees around him all the while moaning.

V I I I

Nola

▼

N OLA HAD FORCED THE FOOTSTEPS and hoots and cries of Miss
Marius's household far from her mind, and she flinched
when Miss Marius opened the door and walked into the room.

The two women eyed each other for a long minute, each
respecting the strength of the other.

"What did you come back for, Nola?" Miss Marius finally asked.

"I been asking myself the very same question," Nola said.

"Raisin don't think the answer is her."

"She's a part of it. So is El. And . . . " Nola's voice trailed off
in a whisper.

"Your mama?" Miss Marius asked.

"She's a piece of it too, but it took me staying this month in
Pearl to know that."

"If it ain't Raisin, or El, or your mama, then what you come
back for?" Miss Marius asked again.

Nola scooted her generous behind over to the edge of the bed and watched her yellow feet dangle.

Miss Marius sat next to her and put one of her holding hands on Nola's shoulder.

The two women sat, the older holding the younger, until the young one shivered and was finally able to speak through the years of quiet pain packed inside her throat.

"My mama always used to talk about bleeding. Bleeding for daddy and for me. How she'd make sure she showed him her blood, make sure he knew she was bleeding. Always bleeding for him. I used to cut on myself, take a stick or a sharp pointy rock and try to make myself bleed like she bled, hurt like she hurt.

"She never did want no babies, said she didn't come into this world to be no sucked-up sponge, no grinding rock for the feet of the world, no giving tree, no jailhouse with no free rooms inside herself.

"I used to take my teeth and bite little holes out my skin to bleed. Watch the little red pools shine on my black skin. She used to be mama, then. Before I started calling her nuthin but Ouida. Ouida Barnett.

"She told Aunt Bess she shot my daddy," Nola whispered in the voice of a wondrous child.

"Some say she did shoot him, child. But nobody knows for sure but God," Miss Marius said, solemn as a bell.

"Sometimes I'd dream and see my daddy with a shiny hole in his chest. A big red shiny hole ringed with light. And then I'd see Ouida Barnett when she was still mama and she'd be singing in the dream with that same shiny hole glowing around her mouth. Then I'd look down at my own hands and see them shining, and I could bend my neck down and look into the insides of myself, and see that same red hole.

"That's the only time that girl would cry, Miss Marius. The

only time. When I saw that same hole shining in all of us. I tried once to show Ouida Barnett my own blood, my pain that was red as hers, show her that I would bleed for her too, but Ouida Barnett said, 'No, girl. Can't nobody bleed for me.'

"When I was seven and my daddy died, my mother said my daddy got killed trying to love somebody else's mama. Said somebody shot him to Kingdom Come where he always acted like he wanted to go. Said it was good he finally got to do some bleeding of his own. Said she'd always be grateful to anybody helped him get what he want.

"I kept trying to hurt myself to try to show my mother how much I wanted to bleed for her even though she didn't want my blood, but then a long-legged boy started coming around telling me I don't need to bleed. Not for Ouida Barnett, or nobody else.

"And I loved the boy and tried to keep a piece of him for myself always, by getting a baby. But that boy didn't want nobody having no piece of hisself. That boy didn't even have no piece of hisself to hold onto for hisself. That boy couldn't even hold onto hisself, he wanted to get out of hisself so bad.

"So he did. He got out of hisself and left me still trying to bleed and hold onto the wrong thing."

"Didn't none of us know how to hold on to all of our self, Nola. None of us. That was the way we learned how to love, by giving all of our self away," Miss Marius said.

Nola acted like she didn't hear Miss Marius's soothing words.

"I got tired of trying to bleed for people that didn't even want my blood. I tried to stop bleeding, but it was too late. The baby was born. And even though my breasts were tight with milk, I knew I wasn't gonna feed that baby, wasn't gonna raise up no other girl waiting to bleed for somebody else.

"That's all I got to show how much I love Raisin. That, and me coming back here to stop the hurting, the bleeding. My mama's hurt, and my hurt don't have to be Raisin's. She only need to bleed for herself.

"In two days I'm gonna leave Pearl and take Raisin with me. I know I can show her some things. How to be. How to be a woman in the world. That's something I brought back to Pearl, a special kind of knowing.

"So I really come back for me, Miss Marius. To pick up all I left behind, and put it someplace we all can rest."

I X

Raisin

▼

WHATEVER'S INSIDE THIS OLD BOX sposed to be from my daddy's grave. My daddy been dead since before I was born and I ain't never seen none of his people. Cept for her. Now everybody talking about my daddy and his people. Bet don't none of em know what they talking about.

Blue think he scary. Ain't nuthin scary about no sposed-to-be wanga-man. Don't care if he do have bones and stuff in old green bottles in his house. Don't care about them old neckbeads. He can't do nuthin to me ain't been done already.

He think this little red box scare me, think all this talk about my daddy gonna make things different tween me and Nola Barnett. He wrong. Ain't nuthin in this world gonna make me go nowhere with that crazy woman.

Gonna tell her. Tell her all I think about her and my daddy and what they both can do. Neither one of em been around nowhere when I needed em. They think they got the right to be

coming around now telling me what they want, what all I'm
sposed to do. What about what they was sposed to be doing?

"Raisin, come on in here. I wanna talk a minute," Miss Marius call from inside the kitchen.

Grown folks always want to be talking. Never wanna be on
the listening side.

"What you got there?" she ask me, pointing at the little red box.

"Something for Miss Nola," I say, hoping she won't ask me
no more about it.

"Well, sit on your sit down a minute. That's just who I want
to talk to you about."

I close myself up inside. Know what she gonna be saying
fore it get out her mouth.

She reach cross the table and take hold one of my hand.

"Now, Raisin, you know I took care of you, raised and loved you
since you was a baby. And you know I'm always gonna love you."

Knew it. I knew she was gonna cut me loose and send me
drifting on the sea of that crazy woman's world.

"But Nola is your mama. And she the only one of y'all's
mamas that come back like she said she would."

"But she come on account of my daddy, not me," I say, raising my voice to fill a hole I feel growing inside.

"I don't know what she told you, child. But I know she come
all the way back here for you. She want to take you back with her
in two days and I want to tell you something," she say, and get up
from the table still holding my hand. She sit next to me. She got
hold of my hand but I don't even feel her skin on mine. Feel like
she talking from the shivery side of a cold dream. That big hole
inside the only thing real.

I look at Miss Marius for a long time. Look at the yellow and
purple flowers of the scarf wrapping her hair like she always got a
present on top of her head. Look at her strong hands on mine,

her dark eyes begging me for something ain't no way in the world I can give.

I close my eyes and feel my head laying on her lap, the smell under her dress a warm, funny perfume. Feel her hands, those wide hands rubbing, stroking my head, the soft cotton of her dress soaking up my tears.

"You the only mama I care about, Miss Marius. You the one. Not her," I say into the white light of air that was squeezing inside me till I felt like a old rag stuffed in a hole in a wall somewhere.

I keep my eyes closed, feel the warmth from her body touching me inside like a flame shiny with hope.

She hold me then. Inside her soft, mighty arms. Hold me for a long time without saying a word.

I feel myself sinking, into a deep space. A black space. No ground under my feet. No sky over my head. Just black. I go down and my body don't keep a shape. I float in a hole in a wide black space. No heart. No skin. No body. Just bones.

Her words follow me down.

"You ain't never gonna be free of your hurt, baby, till you learn how to take your mama inside yourself. You gotta learn to forgive her. Right now, you can't see how to do that, but one day you will. Now you want to try to cut her from you, like you feel she cut you from her. But it don't work like that.

"You gonna get grown one day. Make mistakes of your own. You keep holding onto what your mama didn't do and what you wish she woulda done and your whole body gonna swell up with bitterness and spite, and all you're gonna have for the rest of your days is excuses for your mistakes instead of standing behind the things you end up doing in your life.

"You won't ever see the good your mama give you. You won't never grow up inside. You'll always go around like a piece of you missing. You won't see that you could cut off your child, if you have a child one day.

"But what should make all the difference in the world, is your mama come back for you. After all these years. And don't none of us know the price she paid for staying away. Don't none of us know the price."

Miss Marius press her lips against my cheek and leave the room. After a while, I get up and set the red box outside the door to Miss Nola's room.

X

Raisin

▼

RAISIN LOOKED AT THE DARK BROWN STAIN on the white cotton drawers she held in her hands. Though she washed them again in the washtub, the stain reappeared.

Miss Marius would know something wasn't right, soon as she saw all the dripping white drawers hanging on the clothesline back of the house.

Raisin wondered if the bleeding was ever going to stop.

She jumped as the door to the room she shared with Wilhelmina, Douglass, and MC opened and Lucille stepped into the room. Raisin dropped the panties on the floor.

"What you got there?" Lucille asked.

"None your business," Raisin replied.

Lucille walked slowly over to the bed and spied the stained underwear on the floor.

"I know what this is," she said with a wicked grin. "You better not be messing with that dumb boy, Sin-Sin."

"Ain't none of your business."

"It'll be Miss Marius's business though, and your mama's. Bet she won't be going around talking about taking you nowhere with her, she find out you messing around with that boy now you got your blood."

"Ain't nobody gonna find out nuthin, cause I ain't messing around with nobody."

"You watch," Lucille said, turning to leave the room. "Thinking you Big Hat now cause of Nola Barnett. But you still ain't nuthin but a old ugly wrinkled-up raisin don't nobody want."

Raisin grabbed Lucille by one of her big arms. "Don't go butting your big head in my business."

Lucille turned, shrugged Raisin's hands off her arm and grabbed Raisin's neck. She pushed the air out of Raisin's throat with her big thumbs. She didn't let go till Raisin slipped to the floor.

"Ain't nuthin ugly as you got no business," Lucille said as she stomped out of the room.

Raisin lay on the floor of the room she shared with the other children, the other broken children, marked children, given-up-on children. She heard the cracked sound of their laughter out in the yard below.

She lay on the floor breathing harder than she'd ever breathed in her life, slowly easing air into her pulsing lungs.

She tried to see her future as she lay there, gasping. She couldn't make out any shape in the wide space of the black hole she lay inside, couldn't see herself anywhere.

Miss Marius's large warm face flared briefly, a fast burning star. The faces of those she had known and loved all her life danced brightly before her eyes, Nathan, Wilhelmina, Douglass, and MC. Even Miss Dubois and her dumb son, Sin-Sin, passed before her eyes like a ring of luminous beads, before their radiance, too, dimmed.

She thought she saw the curious face of Blue weeping.

Somewhere, deep in the darkness, where once her belly must have been, a small sun blazed. Raisin reached her arms down to touch her belly, reached her thin fingers into the V of her legs, drew back fingertips laced with blood and opened her mouth to release an old scream.

X I

Sin-Sin

▼

O N THE SECOND NIGHT, Sin-Sin rose from the pit in which he lay buried. A winged man stood over him with his face painted white, chanting. Sin-Sin tried to speak, but his mouth was filled with a crystally substance.

"From EyeMe," the winged man said after he finished his chant. He poured water into Sin-Sin's mouth.

"You will dance now. Dance until you speak the words of the spirits."

From somewhere out in the black of night, a low smooth pounding began. The winged man began to shuffle slowly around the pit.

"Dance," he told Sin-Sin.

Sin-Sin began to move like the winged man, flapping his arms and stomping his feet. When the winged man picked up a long stick and began beating the ground to the rhythm of the pounding, Sin-Sin picked up a stick and beat the ground.

Around and around the sacred ground they danced. They danced until the sun went down and the moon came up. Until Sin-Sin could not remember what it was to long for sleep. Until his body glowed from a film of water, and his legs no longer felt like braces beneath him.

Still the winged man danced. And Sin-Sin danced with him until his young body shook with the violent emotional force of a man.

X I I

Raisin

▼

RAISIN STOOD AT THE EDGE of the black pool of water, shivering. The lake was the space she was floating inside, real, spread before her eyes now like an answer to one of Miss Marius's prayers.

It was cold in all this vibrating space, this deep inky watering place. No sky above, no ground below, just endless magnificent black.

She looked into the water, but could not see her reflection. She remembered the story Nola Barnett, her mother, had told her about the healing stone.

"Bet it was at the bottom of a lake just like this," Raisin said as she took off a sock and shoe, then stuck a big toe into the water.

The coldness of the water made her warm inside. She took off the rest of her clothes and laid them in a pile near the water's edge, only keeping on her panties, now bespangled with blood.

She laid her nearly naked body in the soft mud near the lake's edge and closed her eyes. From a great distance, Raisin heard a hissing whisper, "You are sleeping to dream, to die."

She tried to open her eyes.

"You are waiting to be born," the hissing continued. Behind her eyes Raisin saw a great snake-haired woman rise from the surrounding darkness, her yellow eyes unblinking. Raisin looked into the watery glow of those eyes as the woman moved slowly through waves of shadows, a long slick S in the wet dark. The woman moved close to Raisin with arms outstretched as if to embrace her; instead her serpentine locks held Raisin as they slithered across her damp buttocks and wrapped around her legs, before crawling to her waist where they circled its narrow expanse like a copperhead bracelet. Raisin was not afraid.

The woman's snake hair continued its sinuous crawl, past Raisin's stomach, until it rested as one great triangular head between the soft flesh that would one day be a woman's breasts. Raisin looked into the bottomless eyes of the woman, this great snake woman.

The snake woman opened her mouth wide and sucked Raisin into a red darkness. Raisin heard the swoosh of rushing water, of wind creasing the earth in wide moist ropes. She was in a tight space. A long narrow twisting place. Inside a blackness darker than dreams. She pulled herself to a squatting position, then climbed forward on her hands and knees.

She crawled along winding paths, past narrow ledges, through slippery passageways. She crawled over surfaces rough as crushed grains, smooth as the belly of God. She crawled over stones that cut into her flesh like broken beads of glass.

She crawled until her eyes could not see and her lips tasted like tears. Until she could not distinguish the rise and fall of her trembling arms in the dusk surrounding her. Finally she stopped. The narrow space opened into an echoing cavern. An old woman's black face shined red in the darkness before her.

"The snake will not appear without blood," the old woman chanted.

Raisin looked at the palms of her hands, felt the angry pulsing skin on her knees.

"No," the old woman said, shaking her head. "A woman's blood."

Raisin sat in the soft earth of her dream, confused. The old woman motioned toward the V between Raisin's knees, the panties sprinkled with blood.

The old woman moved toward Raisin with a deep wooden bowl. Inside was a paste of red ochre.

"This is the blood from our Mother's vagina. It was made strong with our song."

The old woman painted Raisin's bare torso and limbs with the red wash.

"It is your womantime. You must go deep inside yourself now and make yourself strong. Make yourself pure. Feel the holy river that will flow inside you now. Cleansing you. Making your spirit strong in the sacred blood of our Mother. The earth, like you, has her own womantime. Listen to her, she breathes like you do. Feel how she moves like the blood in you moves. This is the rhythm of life."

The old woman guided Raisin to the outermost edge of the cave and pointed her gnarled hand toward the heavens.

"The moon is like a woman. She swells like she is about to give birth, like you will one day give birth to children or ideas that can help shape the world. She gets cut and heals herself like you will each month.

"Sit now in this moonlight and talk to the moon, ask her to be a balancing wheel in your life. Talk to our Great Mother, pray with your body beneath this bleeding, thinking moon. This is the time to listen to your mind, your soul. Feel all of your body exactly as it is and love her as she carries you in the rich drift of her blood from world to world."

Raisin sat on a mat wrapped in the warmth of the fire. The old woman approached her again, with a smoking bowl of deep red sauce in her hands.

Raisin held the bowl to her lips and drank the bloodlike sauce. The old woman clapped her hands, a loud sound, and then, below that, Raisin began to hear a faint wailing farther inside the black of the cave.

"Your sisters," the old woman said.

A group of wailing black-skinned girls moved forcefully from the darkness, their bodies glowing with the sheen of red ochre.

The old woman began to sing:

We are women of the snake, the moon
Our blood is the essence of all living things
We are flowers, we are trees
We shed our skin like snakes, the moon
We heal our own wounds and make beautiful scars
We spout from both mouths with our womanly flow

The black girls painted red began to dance, they moved their bodies slow and full of grace, they shuffled their feet as they swayed from side to side.

"You are pledged to your fellow women in a vow of our divine blood, a vow more binding than marriage," the old woman called out to Raisin, still sitting on the mat on the ground.

The girls began to spiral, to undulate, circling around the old woman like snakes.

Raisin entered the dancing, the circle of women, and the girls smiled as they danced, gleaming. Raisin began to twist her body, she felt a snake of light move from the dark earth into her dancing legs, then up her spine.

Raisin looked at the old woman, the red-bodied dancing girls. She looked at the blood on her own legs and smiled, then danced alone, toward the great black lake.

X I I I

Sin-Sin

▼

THE CLEARING GLOWED with a misty orange light. He and the winged man walked inside the door of the little house in the clearing.

"Sit," the winged man said.

Sin-Sin sat on the cold, smooth dirt floor.

"In a moment I will give you the cut of a man. And a cut like a woman. You can become a man only after you become whole. There must be a union of both man and woman there inside you, like those total beings, our he-she gods."

Sin-Sin and the winged man walked out of the small house. Sin-Sin and the winged man walked to the foot of the Firstborn. The great carved face of EyeMe emerged from the bark.

"I will cut you in the name of the gods. The cut will bring forth a strength inside you that is responsible and independent. Stand perfectly still," the winged man said as the trees began a cacophonous hissing.

Sin-Sin watched the winged man walk slowly, surely toward him with the knife Blue had carved for him.

Sin-Sin watched the winged man grab hold of his penis with one hand, while holding the knife in his other hand.

Sin-Sin looked down at his penis laying still as death in the winged man's hands.

Sin-Sin made a move to cup his penis with his own hands.

Sin-Sin reached underneath the winged man's hands to catch his own flaccid penis should it fall.

As Sin-Sin reached to save his penis with his hands, he looked inside his hand-eye in the split second it takes for life to turn to death and saw Raisin struggling beneath the deep dark water of the black lake.

The winged man looked inside Sin-Sin's hand-eye and saw the girl Raisin, there struggling.

"You do not move now even if your mother is dying," the winged man screamed into the black night. "Not even to save your friend."

Suddenly, Blue stepped into the circle of darkness. He nodded to the winged man glaring at Sin-Sin with orange-yellow eyes.

"I'll go," Blue said, and the winged man's eyes dimmed. For a moment the winged man looked very old—old enough to be Blue's father, Sin-Sin's grandfather.

Sin-Sin watched Blue melt into the blackness of the thick hot night.

The winged man cut the foreskin from Sin-Sin's penis in one steady even stroke. Sin-Sin watched with his mouth open wide as the winged man cut a thin line along the underside of his penis. The swiftness of the cutting and the bright shine of his own blood and soft split skin left him much too stunned to cry.

"Now you are a man with a vulva. You are a holy likeness of

our gods. We opened your head so the spirits could enter. You have learned the great secrets of our First Ones. You have learned of the sacredness of human life and the world. You know that you are part of a line of great people and the Night People are the Ones who talk to our first god.

"This cutting is a sacred act performed in the name of our ancestors, our first god. To die by this cutting is to begin the long walk on the road of wisdom.

"And what name do you wish to be called now that you are a man?"

"Kle Goodnight," Sin-Sin whispered.

"From this day forward, you will be called by the name you have chosen, the name of our ancestor, Kle Goodnight."

X I V

Blue

▼

BLUE RAN TO THE EDGE of the calm black lake. He looked for Raisin in the softly moving waves. He stood inside a ring of smooth white stones. The air brushed his warm skin with cool gentle fingers. The pungent scent of another world warmed his nose.

Something in the black water called his name.

He stepped forward, out of the circle of rocks, into the light of the lake's pale aura.

The water kept whispering, whispering his name.

He moved closer to the water, slid his long feet up to the edge of the water, till the tongue in its black mouth lapped the toes of his worn-out boots.

Blue stepped into the water and stared inside the black mirror beneath his feet.

He saw the twisted face of his mother. He saw Miss Marius,

young and fine, swinging ropes of dark woolly hair, the hint of yellow in her dark eyes when she smiled. He saw Mr. Goodnight laughing with his square magnificent teeth when Blue promised he'd teach others the secrets of their people and could see the pride in the old man's face.

He saw Raisin floating on the soft black waves.

Blue, like his father, did not know how to swim, but he remembered Mr. Goodnight telling him to hold on to his breath and believe.

Blue stepped farther out into the water with all his clothes on, pushed himself forward, into a black watery world.

Holding his breath, he laid in the water, stretched, then kick-walked his way across the surface of the lake, his strong arms pulling himself forward.

He pushed his arms and legs through the water for what felt like miles, but he still didn't reach the body he saw floating.

When his lungs began to burn inside his chest like two pieces of burning suns, he knew he had run out of air.

He thought about Mr. Goodnight as he opened his mouth and breathed dark liquid air. He saw the softened face of his father reaching out his arms to greet and hold him, a blessing.

And then he was spinning, turning over and around, going down into the darkness of another world. The spirit world. Another kind of heaven.

He opened his eyes and saw Raisin struggle towards the shore.

He wanted to open his mouth and laugh. So he did. He took the water inside his mouth in great rolling swallows as he went down into a watery womb, into a black liquid heaven where spirits strolled before Blue's eyes dressed in nothing but the brightness of their own peculiar light, here in this other world, this deep watery underworld, where Blue continued to drop into a blackness the color of dream, where spirits played and laughed and sang again, waiting their turn to be born.

EPILOGUE

Raisin

▼

BEEN THREE YEARS SINCE I come out of that lake and find my
mama there, waiting for me with her arms open wide. Most
times I call her Nola B., though, not mama. She all right. Now
that we know my life ain't hers, or her mama's. It mine.

Didn't wanna come out here. Didn't wanna live in no
wanga-man's shack. But Nola B. say, either we stay at Blue's
place in the woods or we gonna leave Pearl. Tell me to take my
pick. So I do.

It ain't so bad. We got most them old wanga things out and
fix the place up some. But Nola B. still won't take that musty-
smelling horseshoe from over the door. Say it protect us, bring
us luck.

She say a lotta truth in things Blue used to say and do. Say
he the one pull me back from them black arms under the lake.
Say he the one take her to the spot in the woods where my daddy

let his spirit go. Tell her she the one gotta make peace with the spirits, not me.

She say what was left of my daddy's bones was inside the little red box. Blue tell her to add some roots and water to the dust inside the box and then sprinkle the mix on my daddy's grave. Say the Night People would come and take the mix away so my daddy's soul could be free.

And I don't forget what Blue do to Sin-Sin, turning him into a man and all.

"Septeema, come here," Nola B. say one night, soon after we start living in Blue's shack. She still don't call me Raisin.

She got a little jar in her hand.

"Get that frown off your face, girl. This ain't nuthin of Blue's," she say, and laugh. She make a motion for me to take off my clothes.

"Got something for your skin," she say, like that little jar hold all the promise in the world.

Don't wanna take off my clothes at first, but slowly I do what she say. She got white candles burning on the bureau in the room we share. Every now and then we sleep in the same bed. It kind of like sleeping with MC and Wilhelmina and Douglass, but it different. Those nights she hold me and whisper and sing soft in my ear till I fall into a dream. Some nights I hold her.

So this what a mama is, I say to myself—a soft warm holding place, a round dark-smelling wishing place, safe as a womb.

She take her strong fingers and put the wet paste all over my body.

"Crushed comfrey leaves," she say. "Help take the wrinkles out your skin."

Didn't believe them leaves was gonna do nuthin for my wrinkles, but I let her put them on me most every night. After a while, my skin start loosening up, smoothing out a bit.

One day, Lucille see the change in my skin. She one of them fast-tailed gals always fanning their behinds around boys at school. She even fan her tail around Sin-Sin. I act like I don't even see it.

She call me out in the schoolyard. "Got some wanga put on you or something?" she say, laughing nasty-like. Seem like everybody ever been born looking at me standing in the yard with my face getting hot.

"Raisin putting swamp-water on her face at night," she keep on. "Out in the woods drinking chicken blood with her mama. Think somebody gonna think she pretty."

I look in Lucille's mean mean eyes thinking I'm gonna see two devils inside, but what I see instead is me.

"She better than pretty, Lucille," Sin-Sin say, walking up on us, "she interesting-looking."

Sin-Sin talking to me for the first time since Blue die.

We walk quiet down the road toward home. Don't ask him why he don't speak all this time. Don't ask him if he blame me about Blue drowning.

"How's your mama?" Sin-Sin ask.

He act like ain't no time passed tween us. Like that night in the woods never happen. Like Blue's spirit ain't walking down the road with us.

"She fine, how yours?"

"Good. Good," he say, then silence. After we walk a way, he stop and say, "I just wanted to talk to you before I go."

I stop walking too and look in his face. Orange-brown boy-man face. His eyes don't got that gimme-look inside like the other boys got.

"Where you going?" I ask.

"Down to stay with some of my mama's people in Louisiana

for a while. Going to college down there. Blue always say a man gotta learn all kinds of things, all kinds of ways, so I'm gonna do some of that. Going to learn some more about things Blue tried to teach me from some other men like him."

"What kind of things?"

"About plants and things. About the old ways of doing things, old ways to be."

"You blame me for Blue, don't you?" I ask.

"Huh?" he ask.

"You think it my fault he dead," I say.

"No. Blue did what he had to do, like we all do," he say.

"Like you gotta go to Louisiana."

"Like that," he say and smile. "I thought you thought I should've got you out of that lake instead of Blue."

"Huh?" I say.

"Since all the time I was running around talking about being a man, I thought you thought I was a coward cause I almost let you drown."

I look at him and laugh. Shake my head. Tell him, "I don't never expect you or no other man to be running around trying to save me from nuthin. I can take care of myself."

"Yeah, well, that's good to know. Next time you might have to drown."

We both laugh. It feel good. Standing in the road, laughing with Sin-Sin.

"You different," I say. "You different now cause Blue done changed you into a man?"

"Naw. I got a ways to go before I'm anywhere near the man Blue was."

"But you ain't like you used to be," I say.

"What used to be missing, ain't missing in me no more. It's hard to explain," he say, then get quiet again. "You know I'll be going by a new name now. Kle Goodnight. You might want to know it for when you write me letters."

I look at him like he crazy. Why he think all I got time to do is sit up in Pearl and write him letters? I ain't none of them tail-fanning gals.

He laugh like he know what I'm thinking. "I'm coming back to Pearl after I learn what I need to know. What you got planned for the next few years?" he ask.

"I don't know what all coming my way," I say. "I ain't but fifteen."

"You got time," he say, and we quiet again.

That evening I sit on the bottom step of the porch tween Nola B.'s legs while she plait my hair in two thick braids. She still don't think I'm old enough to fix my hair the way I want. Miss Marius gonna fix Wilhelmina's hair in a style Wilhelmina saw in a magazine, for when we go to the picture show tomorrow. But Nola B. don't wanna hear nuthin about what Miss Marius gonna do. She just look at me and say she grown and I ain't, and ain't neither one of us gonna be following behind what Miss Marius, or anybody else, say or do.

I lay my head back in her lap and look in her face. Smell the warm musk rising beneath her soft cotton dress. Such a sadness floating inside her eyes, the black pools of her eyes. I see me in there. See me staring at myself, smiling. Her tears drip slow on my face, blessing me, forgiving us for the hurt we will give each other in the years to come.

"I'm glad you come back, mama," I say, and start to hum like her mama hummed, and then she start, and we hum till we turn into one dark body inside the holy sounds.